THE HILLS

THE HILLS

T P NASH

Copyright © 2024 T P Nash

The moral right of the author has been asserted.

Apart from any fair dealing for the purposes of research or private study, or criticism or review, as permitted under the Copyright, Designs and Patents Act 1988, this publication may only be reproduced, stored or transmitted, in any form or by any means, with the prior permission in writing of the publishers, or in the case of reprographic reproduction in accordance with the terms of licences issued by the Copyright Licensing Agency. Enquiries concerning reproduction outside those terms should be sent to the publishers.

This is a work of fiction. Names, characters, businesses, places, events and incidents are either the products of the author's imagination or used in a fictitious manner. Any resemblance to actual persons, living or dead, or actual events is purely coincidental.

Troubador Publishing Ltd
Unit E2 Airfield Business Park,
Harrison Road, Market Harborough,
Leicestershire LE16 7UL
Tel: 0116 279 2299
Email: books@troubador.co.uk
Web: www.troubador.co.uk

ISBN 978-1-80514-545-5

British Library Cataloguing in Publication Data.
A catalogue record for this book is available from the British Library.

Printed and bound in Great Britain by 4edge Limited
Typeset in 11pt Adobe Garamond Pro by Troubador Publishing Ltd, Leicester, UK

For Sarah

CHAPTER 1

May 1973

She would send a card, say what a great time we had, didn't we? When shall we do it again? And don't expect a reply, not straight away. She smiled, a slight cough, looking out of the window, away from other people. She wanted to laugh.

The train was running late. When was it going to get in to Reading? She swore under her breath. Normally, she hated 'fuck' thrown carelessly into conversations, overheard in trains, buses, shops, parks, even university buildings. The rare expletive uttered at home under conditions of deep frustration stunned her family. Called for an apology; an embarrassment. Why did the train have to be late, this day of all days? It was early May and hot, and she felt sticky in that dress; hadn't thought that it would be so warm and that she was going to feel everything so ... physically. No, she couldn't think of that, not now. That would have to wait. She would have to hold it in mind, hold it zealously like a new-born babe, protect it, caress it, hold it close; very close. She had to get home, first.

Didn't she?

It was tempting to leave everything and live her day again hour by hour, the surprise, the mounting excitement, the unexpected words; she didn't want to forget any of it. She was sticking to the seat and sitting on the wrong side of the train in the sun; usually thought of things like that. Not today though. Ordinary things were not important enough to think about. Now she was in the desert, dry and arid, sweltering under an overhead sun, Lawrence of Arabia. At least he had had a robe over his head, whatever it was called; one of the times when you felt jealous of Muslim dress, a cool screen against the outside world.

She tugged at the front of her dress, peeling the cloth off her breasts to let some air in. It had seemed such a good choice that morning, an abstract print, cotton and a real bargain from the animal charity shop in the High Street. Or was it Oxfam?

Now that man was staring at her again. What if she stared at him, stared at his crotch? Would he give up his staring? Or would he become a nuisance? What does one do then? Scream? That would be a joke. She gave up, resigned herself to the sticky heat and looked out of the window. It was smudgy; didn't they ever clean carriages? No sign of life in endless seas of wheat, or whatever it was. So green. What would it have been like to run through? Would it have felt cool, the corn lapping one's naked legs? Wet between the toes, cool.

Naked?

Not the same as bare. More exciting, more essential. Used to run naked round the garden at home, naked as a bird flying over the flower beds, screaming while Dad chased them … couldn't wait to get caught, wrapped up in a bear hug. And then naked at the seaside, strutting into the water, dancing over the waves, water, waves and sand, cool, splashing, cool … the sunny afternoons. Don't see that these days, naked children on the beach. It's all cover-up, and a bit of Ambre Solaire, or whatever it's called.

Daniel had been as white as a jellyfish when he was a student. No, it's not white, is it, more translucent as though you could see right through it. No sun had touched his skin; he was white and thin and pale, all except for his cock … she remembered the Greek island, so quiet, that bay, that long long afternoon, so private. He was shy, he kept going on about these Greek gods, Neptune and Caenis, she thought it was. Something about a ravishing but it was all talk. He could talk all right but she had to wake him up. Move things on. Ravishing indeed. She had to coax him out of his shorts and teeshirt and then rub sun cream all over him, all over. That did it.

Such a bloody long time ago.

Who was she to be having these feelings, today, an ordinary extraordinary weekday when her husband went to work and the children went to school and she went to London for a bit of culture and the day opened like a flower ...

She was a housewife who spent her life cooking, washing, shopping, organising, picking up children, ... she had to face it, she was middle-aged, boring and ordinary. Plain Jane except that she was Mary. Her husband was far more interesting, busy, too busy for her – no, she didn't really think that – and she kept house and home for him, wasn't that the truth? So what had happened? Why did she feel that she could walk on water today, kiss the ticket inspector and still be smiling? If it hadn't been so hot. And when could she get away to London again? How soon? What would happen?

She was out of her comfort zone, flying like a wasp destined for a swat. They were all too clever for her, her dear husband and his friends. What did they talk to her about? Holidays and children; holidays that Daniel couldn't afford and children that the friends didn't have. It was enough to make her scream. And then they turned away and talked about interesting things amongst themselves, history, painting, literature ... Why couldn't they talk to her about painting and music and books and sex ... oh yes, sex.

It wasn't as if she resented Dan's Oxford life. Of course, she had loved seeing his College, visiting the pubs that he had drunk in, his bookshops, even his bedsits and the park where he had walked his first girlfriends, not that there were many of them by all accounts. More friends than girlfriends was the impression. It hadn't worried her that she hardly ever met his friends. What would they have said to her? There she was, a staff nurse, John Radcliffe trained, used to work and noisy chatty drinking sessions with her mates. Not an intellectual thought among them; wouldn't have been right. Didn't do to be academic; it showed the others up. They thought they were clever if they tried the crossword puzzle, the one in the Mail.

And there he had been one night. In the Kings Arms. She didn't know who chose it; not their usual haunt, too University, too clever by far. And they were sitting in the window corner and some boys came up and told them they were sitting in the committee seats. What committee, said Cheryl, all aggressive. And this boy gave them a look and said something to his friends and they laughed and sat down somewhere else and she was for leaving but Cheryl had her hopes on landing a big rugger type, God knows why, and it was her birthday so they went along with her as they always did and stayed. They were never short of boys wherever they went. Something about being a nurse; they were meant to know it all; that was a laugh. The mechanics of it was one thing but the heart of it was another altogether. Anyway, there he was, a northerner like her if Leeds is northern. And sitting on the edge of the group until Cheryl, she thought it was her, dragged him into their group and teased him

… why did she always do that? He only had eyes for Mary from the start, didn't he? The two quiet ones together. Quiet and deep waters; he was her trout turning gently in the shadows of the current; was she the maybug or the fly on the end of the line? Perhaps, she thought, Cheryl had been jealous. Never thought of that before.

Had to get home before the boys. She looked at all those little terraces going by. If she took the roofs off and looked inside, what would she see? Would there be any excitement, she wondered, anything like she was feeling? They looked so ordinary, so grey and domestic and predictable and boring. Boring! And she thought she had been boring. But maybe, in one or two, there was someone who would understand how she felt, someone who had been there and still remembered it all, the buzz, the sense of unreality while casting off mundane duties, making time to go there …

Maybe … maybe it was Daniel's fault. They had been married for years, years of her seeing him into a Professorship while she did years of children, babies puling and throwing up and babyseats and toys and parents' evenings and dirty clothes and holidays. And it had been all right; really, it had been all right, she couldn't say she had loved it but it had come naturally, water off a duck's back Daniel had said. But then, he had never really asked, never wondered whether that was the life that she wanted as he turned away, turned to another session of essays or writing or meetings. And what did she want, all those years?

Why hadn't she thought of all this before?

Ever since Oxford, Daniel had been always too busy, too busy to play with the children except on holiday, too busy to do his share of shopping or washing-up or ... or be with her. He was happy, that was obvious. He had no need to worry about the children or the washing machine going wrong or the car service or the insurance. She had taken care of it all, hadn't she? Taken care of bloody everything? Because she loved him, loved them all. Still did.

But it was a bit like a prison and she was not boring. She didn't have to give up all her life to washing and shopping. She didn't have to wait in bed for Daniel on the off chance. She was floating free, floating on an away-day excursion to paradise. Ooh, that was a bit corny. Better avoid that in her book.

At last, the train seemed to be pulling in. Oh no, an announcement: apologies, 'platform was not ready' for them. They were watering the plants or sweeping or washing the litter bins or something. Perhaps this was the Royal Train and the red carpet was not ready. God, it was stifling in the carriage; she wondered if the heating was still on? Great Western waking late to spring. If only she didn't feel so sticky. Blame ... no. She wouldn't do that. Did she feel guilty? No, she was damned if she was going to feel guilty; she had earned her awayday with all the frills and if it had become something much greater than she had expected, she wasn't going to feel guilty. Only guilty of not being home before the children. And they were coming to an age when they didn't need her all the time, less and less actually. And then what would she do? With all that free time? Years ago, they had talked of her returning to nursing but they both knew that nursing had changed, that nurses all had degrees. And that was something that she did not have.

At last, they were there.

As she jumped off the train, she felt that years had fallen off since that morning, wings on her heels she felt so good. She hummed as she wove her way through the platform crowds – how did people walk so slowly? – feeling the air move around her skin, sweat drying. She handed in her ticket and grabbed the first taxi. What a luxury! She sat back and laughed. Really, she couldn't confess it to Daniel; it had been enough paying for a ticket to Paddington. And the Underground. And … Oh but she had forgotten, she hadn't paid for lunch, or … or anything else. It was not quite rush hour and it didn't take long to get to the University side of town, their side of town, where familiar faces walked the pavements and the clothes and prams and cars were not quite so smart as in some other parts. Sometimes one would think that Reading had never heard of their own university; there had been a student survey the year before that found that only a few knew of the university and so there was a lack of rentable property for students, but anyone could come over to this side of town and see for him or herself.

Home, sweet home. That rainwater downpipe! She had to get Daniel to fix it. She had been asking him all winter. Maybe she would have to do it. She paid off the taxi; he was a bit disgruntled at the size of the tip but she didn't have any more cash.

Home looked a bit like those bored houses that she had seen from the train: a little bigger, a semi-detached instead of a terrace. Come to think of it, it was just like the one that belonged to that tired boring woman who had left it this morning to go and look at pictures in London. The woman who had left the washing, school uniforms, prep to be checked and a teenage daughter with whom one had to negotiate about work, bedtime, parties, clothes ... especially clothes. What had she been like at 14? Maybe worse.

She shrugged with a smile and pushed the front door open.

Immediately she was consumed by the grey cloud of domesticity, the smell of jobs to be done, the taste of cleaning, the memory of cares and demands. Josh rushed to hug her, dear boy. He had the slightly crazed look that he brought home from school; he had not yet worn it off on his toys or his older brother.

'Where have you been, Mummy?' he demanded, bright eyes examining her. What could he see? Could he see her own private pleasure? She was not used to hiding things from those who knew her well. Did she look guilty, pleasure something only to be enjoyed by children? She followed him into the kitchen. Seb was sitting at the table, reading a newspaper. He glanced up nonchalantly and a moment later with interest.

'Seb, dear, have you had some tea? What about you, Josh?'

Seb looked her up and down and she could feel herself beginning to blush; he was only eleven, what could he know about adult life? But he had caught her unawares. She turned away to the kettle and asked if they wanted a drink.

'Mum, you look different!' said Seb.

'Really? Now, have you had tea, anything to eat? Supper won't be until the usual time; I don't know whether your father will be in –'

'What is it? You look different! Doesn't she, Josh?'

'The train was boiling and late. I've had to rush to get back here and I wanted to get back before you got back from school. No sign of Mari yet?'

The boys were not interested in their big sister and they drifted off, Josh to the television and his toys and Seb to his room and homework. She sat down and allowed the day to wash over her, pulling up the memories before they sank under the morass of demands. What had happened, exactly? Were there words said that now she dared not remember? Would her memories create a false theatre, a stage of misunderstood intentions? What a pity that she had had to rush home, cut short their conversation just when things were changing, her whole life turning on its axis. What was she doing? All of a sudden, she felt in no hurry to get supper or even worry when Mari and Daniel might come home. She was changed.

She looked around. The kitchen was familiar, worn and scruffy, in need of new decorations. Why did she feel that it belonged in the past like picking up an old dress that she hadn't seen for twenty years? Upstairs, there were four small bedrooms, one of which was Daniel's study and one the boys shared. Mari's room was a no-go area and officially so was the parents' room but Mari was often borrowing clothes or jewellery and the boys liked to come in on Saturday mornings and sprawl over the bed after they had brought up her breakfast. She knew all these things as familiar as putting on a pair of old shoes. But they felt relegated to the past, a past to which she had to drag herself. And face the fact that things would not change. Not then. Not for a while.

Damn supper; was there anything in the freezer?

Mari came in, head down, slamming the front door behind her. Without a word, she discarded coat, scarf and bag on a chair, went to the fridge and took out a pot of yoghurt. It was her latest fad: a helping of yoghurt three times a day, no tea and no coffee. It excluded her from the bunch of friends who congregated in the town to drink coffee and mingle with boys, teasing and rejecting as they pleased. Mary remembered those days and the girls' cruelty; boys never had the skills to negotiate with girls who were experimenting in newfound skills. She wondered whether things had changed. Mari appeared untouched by it but Mary knew that Mari's life was expanding like the universe and that she, Mary, was a smaller and smaller part of it.

'Hullo, darling. How was school? Anything interesting?'

There was no reply. She didn't feel like trying harder.

'Have you anything to wash? I must do the laundry tonight,' she said.

'No. Oh, could you do my tracksuit? It stinks, covered with mud from last term.'

'Why didn't you give it to me? When do you want it by?'

Seb appeared, aiming for the biscuit tin. He glanced at his sister, apparently weighing up the chances that she might actually listen to him for once.

'Mari, did you see? Mum looks different. What is it?'

For the first time, Mari looked at her. Mary held her gaze for a time and then sipped her tea.

'I can't see anything,' said Mari.

'But she did when she came in. Sort of younger. Smiley.'

Oh, the perspicacity of the young! Mari shrugged and left the kitchen. Seb, losing an ally, disappeared. She sighed, partially from relief. And started to prepare supper in the expectation that Daniel would appear, expect to eat and disappear again to some student seminar or local party committee meeting. What should she tell him? What would he listen to?

If only he didn't work so hard. He was a Professor at the University, a good job with tenure, time to do research. But he was too keen, too ready to help out others. Often home late after helping some student with an essay or a young Fellow with research or doing some office work that he had put off to the last moment, reports, forms, files. Mary was not comfortable at the University; Daniel knew that. So many of the wives were intellectual themselves, educated and demanding. Not surprising that the divorce rate was so high among them. The men all worked too hard and the wives got bored and expected more. But honestly, what can she talk about with them? She was sure that they looked down their noses at her, knew that she never went to university and ignored her. What they did talk about? Philosophy, statistics, or how bad their periods were? Oh, to hell with them all. She had a few friends from the school gate and the past but she didn't fit locally; she knew that. Town thought she was gown and gown thought she was town.

The local Labour Party had their hooks into Daniel. She could kill them; they would never get her vote. Always turning up or demanding his presence. She thought that they survived on the papers he prepared for them. She didn't think there was a clever thinker among them. And look at Daniel; overweight from lack of exercise and always scruffy in spite of her attempts to smarten him up. Not a thought for his appearance and not much for his family. It was stupid, really. He did have other interests: pop music and the guitar. They would all love to hear him playing music, having a good time at home. She wondered how much he thought of home and family; she had no idea. Did he feel lonely or did he make new friends, intimate friends, at the University?

It was suppertime; the boys had appeared and she could hear Mari making a great deal of being busy, doors slamming, stairs pounding, making sure that she arrived at the table last; it was a matter of pride, of growing independence that Mary didn't begrudge her. Daniel had come in, grunted, disappeared for a while up into his study and come to the table. He was not meeting her eye, pushing his cutlery around as though he was operating some agricultural implement. Now and then he hummed, a vague sound without continuity. Something was going to emerge; she would have to wait to hear it. But first, the boys started on some long description of a story going round the school about a new teacher who taught French and had just come from Paris and what she might have bought there; a little dirty, harmless banter.

Nobody helped her put the food on the table; nothing new, but the boys always cleared, with a little prompting. Mari had managed to exclude herself from being involved; Mary would have to do something about that at some stage, so that Mari could look after herself at university.

Mari looked a little shocked at the boys' chatter and pulled a cloak of boredom over her; she had nothing to say of the day, couldn't wait to be released from the table. With a show of nonchalance, she said, 'I'll be out for a little while after supper. Got to see someone about homework.'

Mary was about to ask questions, to show concern while seeming not to pry. She often thought about her daughter's life, comparing it with her past and knowing that it could not be at all like her own youth. The young people that she had met seemed to have different priorities which would have been seen as boringly adult when she was still a child. Without exception, they all seemed to be a lot richer than she had been. Before she could say anything, the table was cleared and the boys were off with a scraping of chairs, bouncing off each other like a brace of puppies.

'Seb,' she called. 'Have you finished your homework? Daniel, I wish you would take more interest in your sons' education.'

This was unfair; she knew that he did think about it, now and then. But just then she wished that he would lift all the responsibility off her. Why should she always have to carry the burden of responsibility, run the family while her precocious husband flowered at the University?

Daniel said, 'That reminds me. There's a concert on Saturday night. Clapton and Limehouse Lizzy. They are a Thin Lizzy tribute band. Do you remember? They are pretty good. It was in the paper ... well, Mari found it.'

She was not surprised; Daniel was not organised. She changed plugs and fuses and did small house repair jobs, Mari helped with finding things, the boys cut grass and wood. She wondered how he managed at the University where all life seemed to sprout from programmed demands. She felt angry, briefly, unable to resist provoking him.

'The rainwater pipe by the front door; it's leaking. You told me that you would deal with it weeks ago. It's still leaking.'

He looked at her; she wondered what he was thinking as she waited for the usual weak excuse. She had already decided to repair it, replace the cracked section where one of the boys had crashed into it fleeing from his brother's fist. But tonight, she felt frustrated, unable to let the matter rest, to live in peace. He looked as if he was thinking about something else altogether, some great philosophical theory to be pored over or some radical historical argument.

Before he could reply, the boys swept through the kitchen, Josh brandishing a book while Seb reached for it, occasionally landing a careless blow on his brother's back. Josh was laughing. Mary sighed.

'Mum,' said Seb, 'I need it for my prep and Josh is just trying to annoy me.'

'Give.' Josh dropped the book on the table, turning to face his brother, a cloak of false courage from a parental presence.

She looked at the book; it was an encyclopaedia of space, illustrated with descriptions of historical travel and projections of the future.

'What subject are you working on, Seb?'

'English.'

'English?'

'Yes, I'm writing an essay, sort of a story, about colonising Mars. You see, there's this –'

'Yes, ok. Josh, you can do without the book this evening.'

Josh grinned and danced out of the room.

Everybody had gone. The dishes demanded to be dealt with, the table wanted to be cleared, the washing-machine begged to be filled and all the little things that had stood still while she was in London chattered at her, making demands and wouldn't let her go. She stood still, a plate in her hands, tasting each part of the day. She wondered whether to weep; it would be comforting in some vague way. Didn't she deserve more? To weep would be like washing over the foundation stones of her life. The moment passed and she went upstairs to check on Seb's homework, ask Mari where she was going and collect the dirty washing before returning to the kitchen.

Mari had disappeared.

She remembered the words of Mari and Daniel.

Daniel was standing in his study, staring at a student's essay with a look of frustration.

'Where is Mari? I am not happy.'

Daniel frowned, gazed at the floor and squeezed his hands in his pockets. She hoped that he was trying to remember what Mari had said. And what he had said. Minutes passed. She is not going to let him off the hook; it was always left to her to worry about everything. Not tonight. He looked up.

'Why are you not happy? What can I do?'

'Do you know where Mari is?'

Now she was gritting her teeth, clenching her fists. She wished she could walk out of the room, out of the house, called a taxi and be elsewhere. Back to London. She couldn't. She fought with angry tears, determined not to give in or to seem manipulative. Daniel, his mind full of music or the essay or something, gave a brief laugh, coughed and wriggled. He was trying to be elsewhere too. It was an old game which they had played many times. She would discover some lapse of duty by Daniel, punish him verbally and eventually attend to it herself. Occasionally, she would weep so that he went red with guilt and grinned, an embarrassed weak grin. She adopted a stony face, looking over his head; she felt weary, exhausted by home life.

'I expect she's round at a friend's house. Now, I've got a paper to –'

She couldn't let him go. She shouted at him, 'You know where she is, don't you?'

Daniel leant over his desk, ducking as though she might hit him. She never had; it was an automatic reaction. Suddenly he sat up with a half-smile.

'She mentioned staying over somewhere, I think. She was helping me with tickets for the concert –'

'Staying with whom? Really, Daniel, don't you think we ought to know where our daughter is? She's only fourteen. What concert?'

Daniel twisted away from her. 'I told you, it's tomorrow night. Clapton's playing, with some group called Limehouse Lizzy and I thought that we –'

'Did you remember that we are meant to be out to supper at that damned Labour Party agent's house? I never like going there, and now you've ...'

She heard herself shouting, going into a morass of emotions because her day was boiling away into a boring domestic tangle. By bedtime, she would be struggling to reassemble the memories of London, the intense feelings, who said what, who had done ...

'Oh no! But it's Clapton, and ... could you ring up and say that I'm not well?'

'Do your own dirty work! I don't mind missing the supper but where is Mari?'

Daniel frowned at his desk as though seeking the answer among the mound of essays, papers, books, and CDs. Relief poured from his face.

'Rachel's. She said something about a party ...' He faded into silence.

She saw from his face that he knew that he had said

too much or too little. She attempted a withering look of scorn; it had worked in the past but tonight she felt too tired to act the part.

'A party? On a weekday? Do you know anything about it? No, of course you don't. I'll ring up Rachel's Mum; or do you want to? ... No, I thought not. It's not the weekend and Mari should be home. But you'll have to get yourself out of that supper party.'

She turned on her heel, a little relieved and feeling stronger. Typical Daniel.

Later, much later, they were in the livingroom, watching the news and the end of the day fade, becoming too lethargic to stir. She looked around. The room looked as tired as the rest of the house, as tired as she felt. Her frustrations were dulled by fatigue but a small flame of excitement burnt deep down, a flame that wouldn't be quenched even by Daniel in his present mood, buried in his paper. She looked at him. Poor man ... no, she had had enough. She wanted some reaction, response, anything other than the usual slow draw to bed and oblivion.

'When shall we get away again?'

Daniel didn't stir, didn't lift his head.

She said, 'I love it at Keswick, you know, and your father is so good to us. Can we get away for a weekend?'

Daniel yawned. 'It's a very busy time of the year, you know. Exams and marking, Mari's first GCSEs, boys' year exams and all this damned local party stuff.'

'Matthew was telling me how the hills always

make him feel good, how he can leave all the daily worries behind and walk them off in the hills. And you; I've noticed how you are less stressed when we've been up there. We could do with spending some time together.'

'Can't it wait for the holidays? Only a couple of months.'

'Why do you do that?'

'What?'

'That putting-off thing.'

'What's the matter? You're not usually like this. I must go to bed. Coming?'

He had got up, thrown the newspaper down, anywhere, and was making for the door. She stood between him and the door, staring at him. He looked confused.

'No, I'm ... Oh God, Daniel, I never see you in the evenings now, you're always working or writing. What about your family? Why can't you –'

'It'll be summer soon. Let's try and get up there in July; beat the crowds, take the children camping.'

'Just put it off, you mean? Damn it, Daniel, what is our life coming to?'

He stared at her, a look of genuine surprise. Was her anger and guilt overflowing? Damn it, she was not going to feel guilty. She deserved her own life.

She said, 'I was in London today, went to the National and a few galleries.'

Daniel relaxed. 'Oh, lucky you. I'm so glad; you

should get away more often. Did you see anything interesting?'

He was moving around the room as though manoeuvring for the door, avoiding her eye. She wondered if he was absolving himself, creating a space for her so that he could pursue his own interests that took him away from family.

'Yes,' she said, staring at him. 'I met Elizabeth for lunch and she suggested that we make a regular thing of meeting in London, going to galleries and so on. I might be back late occasionally.'

He had escaped, drifting out of the room, murmuring 'very good, very good', as he fumbled in his pockets, frowned and disappeared.

She carried on talking to an empty room, sifting through the conversations of the day in her mind. Later, she found him standing in his study, headphones on, swaying to music, his hands thrumming out a syncopated rhythm on his legs. She knew where he was, on a stage with Hendrix or the Stones or possibly Lightnin' Hopkins, a rhythm guitar weaving in and out of the melody, eyes closed, ecstatic. Bugger it, she thought. My form of ecstasy would be to escape to a Friday night flight to the Valley of Desire, join the ladies on the soft grass, sexual attentions, utter freedom. Or to slip out of time onto the Moon to walk with Armstrong, shuffling through the dust of millennia, or to spin out to the furthest extents of the solar system, brushed by the Kuyper belt.

'Shall we go to bed?' she said.

'Be with you in just a minute.'

In bed, she lay in that space before sleep, her mind lifting away from her body. She dreamt of being away, away from cooking and washing and being a housewife. She imagined flying free of her responsibilities, watching them fall away like unwanted clothes leaving her naked and clean above it all, desirable and desiring, soaring ...

The next day, when entirely alone, she stripped off her clothes and sat at her desk, in her knickers and bra. It was hot. There was so much to feed into her writing, such fulfilment. In a daydream, she remembered the feelings, creating memories of who had said what and what they had done. And then she started writing.

It came easily, naturally. Her heroine, removed from a past time, found herself in the London Streets, West end, the object of curiosity. And yet, as she looked around, Shura recognised some of the dresses, throwbacks to her own place, hints of past greatness. She smiled, strode down the broad streets. So clean. No mud or stones, few tramps and cripples, lying across the road with their begging bowls. But where were the horses, fine glossy beasts and their carriages and their proud riders, arrogant Cossacks or even soldiers, looking down their noses at ...

Mary sighed; was this going too far? She had read a few Mills and Boon, looked at their rules of engagement and picked up a few women's magazines. What were the limits of what she wanted to say, what she wanted to do? What if she described exactly what had happened to her, the feelings? She was still writing fiction, wasn't she, still just a story? No one could suspect her, a quiet housewife in a suburb of Reading, particularly not her family.

She smiled and started typing again. It was all about escapism and she was going to escape again, soon. As long as she didn't talk to anyone about her writing. Not a soul.

CHAPTER 2

March

Matthew phoned them late February: the snows have lifted off most of the good routes, come up for a weekend soon and have a walk with me. Daniel had spoken with him, he'd said yes, we'd love to come. Walk a little. He told her. There we go, she thought, Daniel trying to please his father again. All right, I know he is a widower, bless him. It's lovely to see him, spend time with him, go into Keswick; we've only done it once since he moved there. But at least we shall get away.

Daniel and Mary were not keen on hill walking. In fact, they were useless, quickly exhausted, unable to keep up with their own children. They preferred a gentle wander into town, a café and a good bookshop, a quick scout round the clothes shops with Mari (if she felt like it), and back for tea. That was a good weekend, relaxation and a little stimulation, followed by a good bottle of wine. Sometimes, she felt that she should drink more simply to prevent Daniel hogging the whole bottle.

One day soon, she thought, we'll send the boys off walking with Matthew; they are dying to explore, get lost on the hills, wander around in the bogs and rain up there. Where Matthew says it's so magical. Perhaps he is seeing the fairies rising out of the bogs, the ones in the local folk tales. He talked about being in the hills as a form of therapy, a place where he found peace. The boys; they're a bit young at the moment. Give them a couple of years, they can go with him and Daniel and I can take it easy. The children love his company; it's always the same with grandparents, isn't it? None of the responsibility and all the fun. Well, if he is taking them up on the hills, he will have to be responsible for them. Until they're old enough to be responsible for him.

Later, Daniel had suggested that they take Edward and Elizabeth and leave the children at home.

'What?' she said. 'Not see their grandfather? They love to spend time there, you know they do. And it's not as if they get to see him often. Only once in fact since he moved to Keswick.'

'And we see Edward and Elizabeth so seldom, I miss their company,' said Daniel. 'It's not as if we are going for long; it will do the children good to survive without us for a few nights. Can't you find a friend to come in and stay? Anyway, I've invited them and Dad says that it's all right. He does have room in the house and I said that we would take some food.'

And that was that. She fumed a bit, wanted to kick him for not asking her. And she had to admit it; she didn't love the company of Edward and Elizabeth even though they were old friends of her husband, university friends. The two Es. Edward too arrogant for his own good, Elizabeth smart, clever and just a bit remote. Couldn't understand her. Known them long enough but never felt close to her; it wasn't that she was snobbish or anything but she seemed to live in a different world. Unrecognisable. Like a foreigner. She should have objected, made it difficult for Daniel. Now she had to think of food to take; she supposed that the Es would drop into Harrods or something if Daniel had suggested they bring anything.

'Are they bringing food?'

'I can't remember whether I mentioned it. I'll give them a call later.'

'Daniel, are we taking them in our car? Doesn't it need a service and cleaning out and when is the MOT due?'

A naughty ploy. She maintained the car; Daniel wasn't interested and had little use for it. She went shopping, Sainsburys and clothes, and filled it, saw it serviced and checked. And she always drove when they went across to Chigwell to see her parents. He might have checked with her, made sure that it would be all right. Mind you, she couldn't help smiling when she thought of the Es sitting in the back seats among the children's rubbish, chugging North.

'No, you are going to have a holiday. Edward will take us in his Jag. A comfortable ride; what do you think?' He was smiling, inviting her to go along with his plans.

She didn't like leaving the children and Edward and Daniel would argue about politics; it wasn't as if Edward knew anything about politics. Except that last year had been quite spectacular with the Watergate break-in and the massacre at the Olympics. Anyone could have views on those problems. Edward just enjoyed arguing with Daniel for the sake of it. It was one of those areas where she was left out. Of course, she wanted him have a good time, enjoy the company of his old university friends but did he ever realise how she felt? Did he know that she was excluded in effect, that they all turned their backs on her and talked about politics or history or people they knew at Oxford and what they were doing now?

She didn't know what she could talk to Elizabeth about. Elizabeth had no children, she didn't know why, but Daniel had suggested that they didn't have time for that, weren't interested and enjoyed a quality of life that would change too much if they burdened themselves with a family. She had asked Daniel if he would have been happier without children but he had just turned away, saying 'don't be silly', and picked up a newspaper.

Of course, Daniel was one of four and Mary had a sister and brother; it made having children inevitable, didn't it? Used to family dynamics. But Elizabeth was an only child and Edward only had one brother much older than him. They didn't have the same feelings about children. Couldn't have. They were nice enough with their brood but it was easy for them; no responsibility, brief periods of playing or teasing, presents in the post, even Elizabeth, who was Mari's godmother. That had been Daniel's idea; she didn't think there was any bond between Mari and her godmother, apart from Christmas presents and Mari's dutiful thankyou letters. Perhaps there would be later on, when Mari had grown up a bit.

But if only she could spend more time with Daniel; perhaps he would start talking about something that might interest her, draw her in, so that they shared a common interest apart from going to rock concerts. Instead, more and more she felt she was going her own way. The children were getting bigger; in four years, even Josh would be semi-independent at senior school. And nobody knew about her writing.

She wanted it that way, didn't want any of these clever academic types butting into her world of fantasy and imagination. What would Daniel's colleagues say if they knew what she wrote? She couldn't put a name to it herself. Sort of SF with a touch of innocent porn; historic with a slant towards romantic. If only she had a bit more experience in the sex bit of it; life had been too hum drum, well, actually rather boring as far as sex was concerned. If only Daniel was a bit more creative, demanding; sometimes, she was afraid of frightening him. She had had to restrain herself early on when she was just waking up, learning a little of what there was to learn. And when she had bought the 'Joy of Sex' when it came out last year, just before Christmas and had left it in the bedroom, hoping that Daniel might pick it up over the Christmas holiday and take the hint, make use of it and be of use to her, he had just laughed, said everyone at the University had a copy, wasn't it good on all the health warnings and stuck it under the bed along with the other books and the vibrator that they had bought when they were young, before children, before important jobs, before they were married possibly. Gathering dust. What the hell did he want? What the hell did he think she wanted?

It was late when Edward and Elizabeth squeezed through rush hour from Islington to get to them. She had supper waiting; they would need to eat sometime.

She had looked at Elizabeth's clothes. Immaculate even for a weekend in the Lakes; she suspected that Elizabeth had gone shopping just for the weekend. Her own old anorak was serviceable; that was about all she could say about it. Old but mainly waterproof except in the heaviest winds and rain. Elizabeth had some sort of chic jacket, zips on the pockets, a French blue cotton sort of material, so light that it didn't stand up by itself like her anorak. And she was wearing jeans; Mary had jeans but she didn't know that they came in that shape, tailored like a pair of expensive trousers. How did she do it? Where did she go to find these clothes? Harrods? She couldn't afford the clothes Elizabeth wore but she would have liked to have asked her about them. What they cost, what they were made of. How she decided what went with what. She might have picked up a few ideas, even a few clothes from charity shops or almost-new to change her wardrobe. Oh well, she would just have to publish a best-seller, somehow. Under a nomme-de-plume that she could never tell Daniel. Or anyone she knew.

It made her sick of her clothes; they all seemed old and tired. Was that one of the reasons that Daniel didn't notice her these days? She would have to think about that. Her own parents never bothered about things like that. She still went red in the face when she remembered her mother's face that evening, so long ago. She was going to a dance with a friend, her best friend from school. And the friend had shown her a dress. She didn't have one of those lovely dresses with the full skirt and tight waist; her mother certainly didn't have the money for something like that. But she had a good skirt, dark blue and full, great for jiving in, and her friend had lent her a top. It was like the one in the photograph of Marilyn Monroe, a black lacy scoop top that showed off her breasts. She had good breasts. Her friend couldn't understand when she turned up late, wearing a school shirt.

Daniel had forgotten his walking boots just as they were leaving. She remembered them in the end; buried in the garage. Still with last year's mud. The children had been fine as if they were going on holiday. She warned them against winding up their carer, a friend; told them that she wasn't used to children, they must look after her. She was speaking to the boys, of course; by that time, Mari had disappeared upstairs into her own world, tired of standing around waiting for her parents to organise themselves.

It was an awful journey to Keswick; Edward's car made her feel sick. Too soft, smoothing its way north. She didn't know what make it was, hadn't meant anything when Daniel had said Jag; something large and expensive anyway. Leather seats that smelt. Carpet on the floor. Radio too loud, until Elizabeth told him to turn it off.

And then, the engine had coughed, once, twice, and died, the car sitting silent on the hard shoulder while Elizabeth swore at Edward; the petrol tank was empty. It was a long wait until the AA arrived with more fuel, a long wait as the car cooled and conversation dried.

After that, they stopped on the way but she felt too sick to eat or drink. Perhaps she should have made a simpler supper before they left Reading. Edward and Daniel started one of their long philosophical discussions until Elizabeth told them to shut up; at least the car was dead silent for the last hundred miles. What a long way.

It was late when they arrived. Matthew was sweet; pointed them to their beds and left them to it. Except for thanking her for the ham and cake that she had brought; he looked a bit surprised but she said that they couldn't descend on him without contributing. Edward brought a case of wine; perhaps he was worried that Matthew's wouldn't be good enough. She hoped that Daniel wouldn't drink too much; Edward always got irritated when he brought a good wine and Daniel drank most of it.

Matthew had registered the fatigue, but welcomed them all as Daniel introduced his friends. Mary looked exhausted; he showed her upstairs and left the others to relax in their own time. Daniel had opened a bottle of wine and offered him a glass but he refused. It was too late, he was going to bed and would see them all in the morning.

The next day was wet; they went for a walk. It took a while to get going; they were sharing the same bathroom. Not Matthew, who had his own but the four of them and Edward spent ages in there while Daniel crossed his legs and Elizabeth got impatient, knocking and calling in her best court voice. But breakfast was wonderful, lots of everything, Matthew looking after them, and Daniel and Edward quiet for a change. Mary had not slept well, too tired, and dropped down in her chair without making conversation. Edward was bubbling, full of questions as to where they would walk, for how long, how high and how difficult; did he need his boots, compass, and all? Should he take a map-case? Matthew smiled, answered briefly, and they set off in two cars. Mary sank into the front seat of Matthew's car and closed her eyes while Daniel questioned his father about Keswick; had it been a good move, did he know people, was the house working out, was he happy? Matthew smiled, assured his son that all was well and how good it was to see them. Was he, Daniel, getting enough relaxation or was work driving him too hard? Mary snorted, Daniel said nothing.

Watdenlath would have been a beautiful place in the sun but it was miserable and it started to hail and rain and blow. They parked under some trees; not encouraging. It was dark, wet and dripping like an old coal cellar. And walked up a narrow valley directly into the wind. Soaked in no time; the wind found its way through her old anorak, under her jersey. Matthew was happy, talking about the rocks and glaciation and walls and sheep and farmers and things, but they spent most of their time with their heads down following the slate path through the fields. No sheep but a noisy stream next to them, roaring down the valley; it made them feel wetter and drowned out most conversation. Hail began to fly towards them, isolating them. She felt as though she was walking alone, unable to talk or even see anybody else. What was the point in all of this? Walking was meant to be fun, not some masochistic form of survival. She had to admit, they didn't walk for very long and she didn't get wet through but it was all unnecessary as far as she was concerned. And they weren't even walking homewards.

At the top of the valley, the tarn was black and dark, reflecting the clouds that loomed over the water. If she hadn't been so cold and wet, she might have enjoyed it, a drama like a gothic film. Or a Victorian novel, perhaps Mary Shelley. Waves broke on the shore in their faces and though the rain had stopped the wind was cold, bitter like winter. Everything was wet. It might be warmer in the water; she liked swimming but in a warm swimming pool; no raw swimming in remote lochs or plunging into the sea at Christmas for her. They sat down on the edge, in the face of the wind with no shelter and ate sandwiches that Matthew had carried. She didn't feel much like a picnic; not her idea of a picnic at all. She couldn't imagine a picnic in that spot anyway. She turned round and huddled, her hands in her pockets, chin on chest. She felt Daniel looking at her and refused to meet his eye. Did he feel as miserable as she did?

Away to one side of the tarn was the little hamlet of Watdenlath; what did the name mean? It didn't look like more than a farm, sheltered by a few trees. A glum place to live, cold and exposed. Matthew said that in the summer, there were crowds of visitors and a tearoom and ice-cream shop open. She couldn't imagine it at all but saw hill farmers, blunt and quiet, turned in on themselves, survivors in a bleak land, sheep their source of food and warmth, their all. And how would their families live? Shops and schools and doctors and ... So remote. An hour to the closest house? And much further to the town. You'd have to be good at dealing with illnesses and setting broken bones ...

They didn't stay long; everyone was getting cold. But Edward would act like a Victorian explorer walking into darkest Africa, blast him, making a show of surveying the landscape, tilting his head back, hands on hips while his bearers brought up the rear. What a poser.

He wanted Daniel to be his bearer. 'Come on, Daniel, let's walk a bit further. Round that hill, perhaps. We could find a way back.'

She stared at Daniel, using all her powers of silent persuasion.

He said, 'No, I'm going down with the others. I need a rest, I'm not as fit as you.'

We ought to get away every two months or so but we don't, she thought; it's not my fault that Daniel is over-weight; I have no idea what he eats at the University. I make healthy food and got a lot of stick from the boys. Even Mari backs me up, from time to time. Not very often.

They turned their backs on the black water, except for Matthew and Edward, who walked on round the tarn. Elizabeth started talking to Daniel and she found herself walking behind them; couldn't hear what they were talking about with the noise from the rushing beck, couldn't join in, just concentrated on following the slate slabs across the little fields. They were slippery. She wondered if she could have a bath when they got back.

She meant to help Matthew get supper. Made the right sorts of noises, looked practical. But Matthew sat her down and poured wine into her until she couldn't stop talking and didn't care what she said. She hadn't seen him for ages; only once since his move from Leeds; it was a bit of a trek up to Keswick. Leeds had been bad enough. He prepared supper, a roast leg of lamb, new potatoes, carrots and peas, cherry pie while talking to her. She was surprised; had he always been this good in the kitchen? Must ask Daniel, how well could his father look after himself. How long would it be before they had to organise Meals-on-Wheels, or something. How old was he anyway? He seemed fit and well.

How were the children? He didn't get to see them very often. He asked particularly about Mari.

'Mari.' She licked the side of her glass to catch a drip and sighed. 'She's 14 now. Sometimes, I don't know, I won't be able to keep up with her for much longer. She's bright, like her father. Does very well at school, we never have any trouble. Parents evenings a formality really. She can argue both of us into a cocked hat. And wrap Daniel round her little finger.'

She sighed and sipped. Time tilted, sliding away from her; she could say anything, feel anything. Free from the criticisms at home; it was the children, not

Daniel. Too clever, always out-arguing her; had to be on her guard, ready with reasons why they must do something or not do something, never relax. Matthew sliced garlic, slim arrows to pierce the lamb; must remember to try that at home. Not that they ever had a good leg of lamb; too damned expensive.

She said, 'Daniel says she must be good enough for Oxford. But I think he pushes her too hard. I'm afraid that she might feel it, resent us. He's already pointing out things that she ought to be reading, novels and newspapers, to broaden her education. I don't want her to miss out on being a teenager. She is growing so fast. You know, the world that she inhabits is so different from mine. Was it the same for you, as parents I mean?'

Matthew laughed. 'I can't remember. Those years seemed so important, education and all. How much was genes and how much upbringing. And now it has all faded away in the past; I've done my time. Mari: she always comes over as such a serious girl.'

'Oh, Daniel is sure that she will get into Oxford; he will do anything to smooth the way into his old College. I don't know … There was no university in my family; I was the first one to do anything. I don't know about university entrance and things.'

Her parents had stood together looking at her final exam results and suggested nursing. It's a respectable job, her mother had said. And interesting. You wouldn't want to be coming into the Water Board like me, her father had said. You're bright, clever. You'll do well at nursing. And who knows, had said her mother, you might meet a nice young doctor. So she had given up the idea of working in the bank with her friend and gone into nursing. And liked it. It was interesting. But she didn't meet a nice young doctor; she met Daniel. And that was that.

'What are you worrying about?' said Matthew. 'Daniel knows what to do. Have some more wine. I'm nearly done here. I didn't ask; are there any vegetarians? I never think of it. They're all meat eaters round here, you know. Mostly lamb, what with the sheep.'

She wasn't listening, remembering the early years, peeling away from Chigwell and her school friends to new friends at nursing school, keeping Matron happy, spending spare time at the cinema, buying a few clothes and dancing. Yes, she had loved dancing as long as they got back in time at night. A way of shucking off all 'proper' manners and being herself. Did her own daughter have pleasures like that, a group of friends walking down the street pushing boys aside, laughing, dancing with boys, kisses in doorways. Did she really know her daughter, where her heart lay. What she thought about. Matthew was watching her; she gave a half smile, apologetic, gathered herself.

'She's always reading, you know,' she said. 'Friends at school of course but doesn't socialise much. At least, I don't think so. Probably a good thing, not wasting her time on cafés and boys. But sometimes, I wonder ...'

'No close friends?'

'Oh, one particular one, Rachel. Goes round to her house though. I don't know what they get up to.'

'What does she read?'

'Do you know, I have no idea. When she was younger, she read all the teen books, you know, Terry Prachett and all the rest but I don't know what she is reading now. She goes to the library by herself. I suppose I should know whether she is being exposed to anything that she shouldn't read. But I don't know; can't imagine anything from the library that would do any harm.'

'I can't remember what the girls read. Or even Daniel, come to that. They seemed to take care of their own reading from about the age of 12; whatever we pushed their way used to sit around and gather dust. What is she interested in?'

'I don't know really. I guess she reads a lot of history and novels from what she has talked about but she's not interested in Politics. I've heard Daniel talking to her about American politics but she ignored him. She's not very sporty. Actually, I think she needs her eyes testing; whenever I have suggested it, she has disappeared or put me off. The idea of glasses, I suppose. But she always appears to be staring at things with her eyes screwed up.'

'You must do something about that, Mary.'

'Yes, I suppose so. It's quite difficult; I don't even get inside her room, you know. She says she cleans it but I never see her doing it. Buys her own clothes and argues with me about the clothes that we buy for her for school. And when I try to tell her what to do, Daniel tells me to leave her alone. She idolises her father.'

'Really? How are the boys? I can't remember how old they are.'

'Seb is now 11 and Josh 9. I sometimes feel sorry for Seb; he is one of those boys who has to work and Josh is sharper. Bullies him. I don't know what to do; I thought elder brothers took care of themselves but Seb feels guilty if he fends off Josh. Oh well, I expect they'll grow out of it.'

'And what about you?'

'Me?'

'Do you never get away?'

What could she say? These discussions always centred round her children or Daniel. What did she do, she wondered through a haze of wine and fatigue. Did writing count as getting away? Into her own fantasy world?

'I ... yes; actually I do sometimes ... You see, my parents used to take me to exhibitions and had art books; quite conventional, nothing modern, but I've always liked looking at paintings. One of the boys, Seb, does quite nice paintings; too early to say, of course. And then we used to go to the theatre quite a bit, much more than these days. Oh damn, I've drunk too much and now I'm talking too much.'

'Here, sit down, there's no rush for supper. Are there any artists you particularly love?'

'Oh yes. Occasionally, I have a day out in London, usually the Cork Street area, and the big galleries, just to keep in touch. Richard Hamilton's my favourite, so daring. And a bit of Hockney, Allen Jones, Tilson. Not so keen on the Americans, you know, Warhol, Rosenquist and all that crowd.'

'Pop Art. I don't know much about it.'

'It's terrific; it's all about today, what we see when we're shopping, driving down the street.'

'What does Daniel have to say about it? Does he like it?'

'We've never really talked about it. I discovered it myself, going round galleries and things. He has never been interested in art.'

'No, he wasn't as a boy. Even though we had terrific art in Leeds. I think he always dreaded the Sunday afternoon trips to the Gallery. His sisters were happier, got more out of it.'

'How are they? We hardly ever see them.'

'They're fine. I'm surprised that Daniel isn't more interested in Pop Art, particularly American Pop Art. I should have thought that it would be right up his street, his interest in modern American culture. I suppose he has heard of that little book by Venturi, the architect designing in a Post-modern way?'

'No idea. He never talks about his work to me. You know, it's not all bliss in an academic's house. As well as his university work, which doesn't seem to have any normal timetable, Daniel has his tutees and works for the local Labour party; some days I don't see him until bedtime. And then the children all have after-school activities; sports, or drama in Mari's case.'

'It's the life of an academic, isn't it? What drives them on. Anyway, it's good to see you; I'm glad you have got away.'

Did he mean from home or from the others?

He was laying the table. 'What's happening at home this weekend?'

'I've left a friend in charge. I hope they get on all right. I'm not sure that she is used to looking after children. The boys will be all right; they'll run circles round her and she will think that they are hard going. But they are not, really. I guess Mari will just take off to Rachel's. She might help with the boys; I think they are both a little afraid of her. She seems to get them to do things when she can be bothered. Oh well.'

'Don't worry. They all strike me as quite sensible.'

'Do you think I might give them a call? It would be a good time.'

Matthew showed her the telephone and left her in peace. It was in a quiet room; he told her that he liked to ignore it ringing when he chose.

The food was delicious, slices of lamb that melted in the mouth, far better than her cooking. She watched Daniel demanding more. Well, tough, she couldn't go buying legs of lamb on her budget. Edward and Daniel talked, always of America but never of the matters that interested her.

'Did you see that old Truman died in December.'

'Funny man. Never stood out, did he?' Edward wasn't very interested.

'Funny position, taking over from the hero Roosevelt. Same as Atlee taking over from Churchill. I guess everybody is glad of a change, particularly in economics. Wars cost.'

Matthew said, 'Oh, I thought that was decided by big business, nothing to do with governments or politics.'

Daniel laughed. 'You're probably right, Dad.'

Mary said, 'Did you see that Apollo 17 returned from the Moon before Christmas? Looks like the last Moon flight for a while.' Moon flights fascinated her; she had sat up in July 1969 to see the first step on the Moon. It fed her writing, not that any of the others knew anything about it. Matthew looked at her, a frown, questioning. Daniel started humming 'Time' from the 'Dark Side of the Moon'.

Edward said, 'Waste of money, all those Moon flights. We're never going to want to live there, or use it in any way. Waste of money.'

'Do you put any value on exploration?' asked Daniel.

'Sure, but only when it looks as if we can get something out of it. Do you know, some contractor spent a million dollars designing a pen that would write in a zero gravity environment to sell to NASA. The Russians use a black wax pencil; costs a few cents, or zlotis or whatever. What do you think of that, Mary?'

Mary ignored him. Edward was being boring, negative. Daniel and Matthew and Elizabeth were sitting in the quiet, enjoying the food that Matthew had cooked, but over there was a black hole called Edward, drawing in matter and energy so that it ceased to exist. Why couldn't he shut up? What was Matthew doing, cooking so well? Had he cooked for the family? He seemed leaner than she remembered, and a different person than the quiet partner to Isobel. Different as though reborn, emerging from a long-term role to find a new life. Hard work, but exciting? How would he appear to a single woman of his age? Would he be attractive (and was that a question of age in any case), and would he be open to another long-term relationship, one where the rules were all changed even down to the side of the bed? How easy was it making those compromises at his age, those compromises that inevitably arose in discussions of food, holidays, education, television, music ... She sipped her wine and wished that she had been more demanding of Daniel.

Elizabeth asked about Vietnam and Daniel and Edward were off like dogs at a track after the electric hare, arguing the downfall of America's presence in S.E. Asia.

'There were advisors in Vietnam in the late 50's,' said Daniel. 'The US was worried about communism spreading into these 'undeveloped' countries. Thought they needed Uncle Sam to sort it out. It's all rot you know. Thank God they signed the Peace Treaty in January. They were getting thrashed.'

'So where will they move to next? Cambodia? South Korea?'

'They've been in South Korea since the war there. Thousands of service men. I can't see them getting out of S.E. Asia in my life-time. Millions of dollars, it's costing them.'

'Yes,' said Edward with a grin. 'They lost a B52 last autumn over Vietnam.'

'How did you know that?' said Daniel. 'Not public information you know.'

'You were speaking of finance; things get around in the world of finance, like the cost of replacing a bomber. They're not peanuts.'

'How much?' asked Elizabeth.

'Oh, I dunno. Quite a lot. And they would replace it with something more modern, more expensive,' said Edward.

'How did you hear?' asked Elizabeth.

Edward ignored her.

'Do you know,' said Matthew, 'when we were in Florence, we never saw Americans, except at the larger piazza cafés, sitting in large groups among their own people. Landladies didn't like them; too demanding, not polite. I saw them walking through a narrow street often, expecting others to move out of their way. Mind you, I had a little trouble myself.'

He sipped his wine, smiled to himself.

'I don't remember you telling us of that, Dad,' said Daniel.

'It was a long time ago, the 30s, before we were married. We were doing the rounds, you know, the list of churches and museums. There's so much in Florence; have you all been there? You really should, you know … and then, oh dear, …'

'Come on Dad. What happened?'

'We were in Piazza di Santa Croce, on the way to Santa Croce. It's a gravelled area, used for fairs and competitions for hundreds of years. An artisan area, full of small workshops, flats over, lively and exciting. We had …'

'Dad?'

'Right. There was a crowd of boys playing football. It was early evening; their shouts were reflected from the buildings mingled with the calls of the swifts catching flies. Dust rose around their feet as they tackled each other. The ball came adrift, rolled to my feet; they stopped, staring at me, gesturing. So I kicked it. We hadn't been together long, I guess I was trying to impress Isobel. I placed the ball, took a short run-up, and kicked. The ball rose elegantly over the boys' heads, bounced off a Fiat 500's bonnet, no doubt causing alarm between the young lovers inside, and rolled onto the top step of the doors into Santa Croce. At that moment, a cleric appeared, all black vestments and black frown. He picked up the ball, wagged a finger at the boys and disappeared into the darkness of the Church.

'The boys were frozen in disbelief; they turned on me, the ineffective nameless foreigner who had lost their ball, and rallied. I looked at Isobel, said let's go, and we ran. Howling like coyotes, the boys gave pursuit.

'Why does common sense depart at times like that? I took a street off the Piazza I didn't know, then a narrow calle, high buildings on either side, no pedestrians, and at the end a cul-de-sac. Washing hung across the alley, women leaning against the walls, chatting, folding sheets. When they saw us, they stared; I don't think many tourists came down that way. They pointed, laughed. The boys were behind us; they had stopped, muttering, shouting claims, complaints to the women who seemed to know them.

'Isobel turned to me and beat me on the chest, tears streaming down her cheeks. "Mama mia, ingrastioso, piccolino, limoncello, salla bagna, basta, fusilli" ... Neither of us knew much Italian, enough to order a drink, say Thankyou. The women joined the boys, pointing at me, shouting, threatening. And then a younger one took Isobel by the arm and disappeared into a doorway. I thought I'd had it. I could feel the sweat pouring off me, down my back.

'An older woman went over to the boys and there was a sort of discussion; the boys were playing the hard-up, not-their-fault act, and the woman was giving them short thrift. She came over to me, making that sign for money. I didn't have much; we were students.

I took out a few notes and she gave me such a look that I took out some more, muttered "studenti … mi …er …sorry.' She shrugged, took the money in her huge fist, gave it to the boys and sent them off with a flea in their ears. The women carried on folding and chatting, ignored me. After half an hour or so, Isobel appeared with the younger woman, bowed, kissed her on both cheeks, said "Ciao"; the younger woman came up to me and gave me a lecture, lots of finger wagging, sharp words. Didn't understand a word. We walked off; well, Isobel took me by the arm and marched me off. In silence.

'Later that night, after we had settled down, got talking, I asked her what had happened. She smiled. She had told the woman that it was her honeymoon, and that I had returned to the bedroom late and drunk last night. She was having a terrible honeymoon, not at all satisfying, her husband was ignorant, crude. She had received a lot of sympathy, a glass of Vino Santo and some advice; it seemed that the woman could speak a little English, had heard that the English were not great lovers. Unlike the Italians, particularly the Firenze. And Isobel said, "if you intend to go on kicking footballs, I'm going home." "It was a pretty good kick, wasn't it?" I said. She didn't say anything. Just looked. She was quite a looker, as I'm sure you remember.'

It was a long evening, mostly discussion between Daniel and Edward, almost always about America and Vietnam. Elizabeth occasionally joined in but was often shouted down by the men. Matthew was content to watch, a slight smile on his face. Mary wished she had asked how he was getting on, how he was getting over the death of her mother-in-law, and settling into Keswick. And all she had done was talk about herself. Although it was early, she said that she was going to bed. The wine and fresh air was putting her to sleep; she swayed as she stood up, looked to see if Daniel had noticed or whether he was coming too. He hadn't seen a thing. To her surprise, Elizabeth got up too and went upstairs with her, talking about nothing in particular, saying that she was glad to leave the men, smiling and taking her arm when she missed the step outside the bathroom door. She was surprised at Elizabeth's friendliness.

The next day, they went for a short walk. Elizabeth was friendly again, walking with her. She assumed that she wanted to leave Edward to have his fill of Daniel, who he didn't see very often. Matthew was quiet and she had a few words with him, asked about his life, but he wasn't very forthcoming. After lunch, they had the long drive south, back to family and home.

CHAPTER 3

April

A few weeks later and we were up here again. He insisted we drove ... could have taken the train, First Class, comfort and relaxation after a week of fighting in Court to win a case for some lout who should have ended up in prison. Got him off; he tried to embrace me. Ugh! His 'uncle', all gold bracelets and floral braces, grinning like an ape, said he would put more business my way. He always had a supply of naughty boys who were getting into trouble with the coppers, too stupid to take his advice. I bet he did. What did he think I was? Some kind of Social Security? Don't bother; I almost said it but you can't. Chambers wouldn't approve. Their greasy solicitor, stained with the fat of his clients, loved our Clerk. Needed a 'leading' barrister, one who was young and fawned to the judge. Someone had to serve an unpalatable sector of the public; what were the Criminal Courts about? Every person entitled to a defence and so on. Would it affect her application for QC? She had no idea.

Friday evening. Needed a little spoiling. Saturday was rest day, a day to live a little. And forget the cases to read and research; that was Sunday night's work. So why was she being borne North on the M1 on Friday rush hour, a motorway full of manic work-crazed drivers seeking escape from London and the South? Edward as bad as the rest, the fast lane at 85 miles per hour, nose to tale. Bugger. Was he looking for an early grave and taking her along with him? Looked at the nearest car: young woman, her age. Blonde, leather jacket, ten-year old car. Smoking, looking at something; a card? 85 mph, heading for an early drink or an early grave.

What was the point of driving like that? Edward couldn't cast off his office aggression, had to push for any advantage, get ahead of the other buggers. You're never ahead, she said. What you mean? he said. Always another car ahead. Yeah, he said, and then you'd never push, never bother to try. It was his practice, those American lawyers, always pushing, always expecting more, only taking on the work that provided big bucks. But what did that do to the workers, the solicitors and their underlings? He didn't used to be like that; could have got a job in the BBC or some newspaper. How long before he burnt out? And then where will we be?

M6, two years old but looks fifty. Crawl past/over Birmingham, elevated above drear factories, roundabouts, workshops, redundant warehouses ... traffic jams, the odd over-heated car forcing us into a single line queue, the aggressive ones pushing to the front. So bloody tiring. Edward used his horn, like a huntsman leading the charge. Not popular with other cars; we were shut out pretty effectively for a while. Which didn't do Edward's mood any good. Silly bugger.

Onto countryside, Edward flicking on the radio, turning it off, turning it on.

Stopped twice, Edward hassling her, no time to relax, always got to go, as though he might fall asleep if he stopped for thirty minutes. Wouldn't be a bad idea, a good sleep. She crawled into the back, curled sideways, pretended sleep for an hour. Crooked back, bad temper. Back in front. And then, around Lancaster, the traffic had thinned, nobody in front of them in the fast lane, the country lifting around them, small fields, stone walls and farms, trees giving shelter and animals, cattle and sheep. The hills that Matthew spoke of as sentient beings. She liked this section of the journey, the change from industry and flat farmland, houses and factories. Like another country, the England in travel brochures and the travel sections of Sunday papers. More restful.

Almost there, light faded in that April evening. The road was forced into curves around great hills that threatened to block them, hold them back, a gateway to another land; they rose high, dark majestic presences on either side. Next to the road, a mountain torrent, cutting through. They climbed above it all to the summit of Shap. And galloped downhill from Penrith to Keswick, Blencathra looming over them in the twilight, a dark hostile being.

Not her idea of a holiday; too rough and rural, too remote and raw. But the hills did look grand, from the leather comfort of the car.

They arrived late.

Matthew greeted them with supper waiting. He seemed younger than she remembered him, fit and a slow smile. The house was neat, welcoming. It smelt of flowers and was quiet. Elizabeth felt tension dropping away and with it became overcome by an easy sleepiness. Edward was swaying a little but his face bubbled with excitement; surely, he was exhausted. It was only a month since they had last been here; Edward had warmed to Matthew who had kindled an enthusiasm for the hills. Daniel, Matthew's son, was no walker. You could see; too heavy, not interested, and Mary was not keen. She had said so. But Edward saw it as a challenge, capturing peaks, pushing on into remote distances, heather, bog, wild birds, rain, exposure. Wilderness. He loved it all. He was welcome to it. Maybe one day he would relax and be happy to be up there without challenges, like Matthew.

Had he ever wanted to walk like that before? He had rowed at Oxford as a matter of form, supporting the College; but he wasn't keen on sport, apart from the odd game of squash these days, keeping up with the fellow competitors at work. The hills demanded a different sort of mentality unsuited to Edward. One that required patience and doggedness, an acceptance of land and weather rather than aggression and conquest. They had had a horrible walk in March straight into hail and freezing wind and Edward had walked further then. Keeping Matthew with him. Matthew didn't seem to mind. Perhaps he would change, adapt to the hills.

Sleep came easily above the murmur of Matthew and Edward talking. And she dreamt of Paris, if it was Paris. A city, eternally sunny, street cafés, interesting people who wore nice clothes, a world where scenes changed around her without collision or stress, a smiling easy world. Of good food, designer gowns, scents, touching, noticing, a glance here, a smile back. Bien coiffée, bien soignée. She smiled and more opened up, enveloping, taking her into other places …

The morning was black. Clouds hung low over the town. She rolled over in bed. Fighting her instinct to wake at half past five. Edward snored beside her; well, he didn't snore but she resented his total relaxation, sleep that resisted the growing light, the spit of rain on the window.

Bugger, no good.

She went down to the kitchen. Was it an old man's kitchen? It wasn't modernised, a world away from her own kitchen. Matthew had only lived there for two years, moving from Leeds a year after his wife had died. She wondered at that; leaving all the old friends behind, all the usual places, banks, library, concert hall and all. To come to a town where he knew nobody, not a soul. Where the facilities must be more limited; she remembered a mass of walking shops, several pubs, a Town Hall dominating the main street, now an Information Centre. What was here for him? How did he spend his days? He couldn't be walking the hills all day. Or even every day. What would life hold for her when she was retired? She couldn't imagine it, couldn't imagine not working, not tackling some case that demanded her skills, her intelligence, a quickness of thought, an openness to think radically, to turn an impossible situation upside down. Work; she loved it. Had to force herself to take time off and the only way was to get away, somewhere entirely different and desirable, accessible, warm.

She looked round the kitchen. It appeared untouched. For twenty years, probably. Formica cupboards, pine surfaces, scrubbed. An old cottage kitchen table, also scrubbed. Plain, neat, tidy – nothing left out. A kettle. The cupboard above – mugs, tea, coffee. Below, the fridge. Obvious. Obviously an ordered home for an orderly man, not one to waste time gathering the essentials together. Did that apply to his life, his acquaintances, the use of his time? Enviable in a way, but also was it a bit limiting? No, how could she judge? She didn't know him well, couldn't judge. And after all, she had no right.

It was a huge contrast with their own kitchen in Islington, cupboards finished with stainless steel, polished Iroko worktops. Little of it used; so many cupboards that she hadn't learnt where things were; left it to the house-keeper. This kitchen must be as Matthew found it, the creation of a former owner. She couldn't imagine doing something like that. Like living in someone's old clothes. The sink looked worn, the chrome wearing from the taps. The Formica showed wear, a few cupboard handles loose, the worktops scored in places. Signs of past users, ghosts in evidence. Was Matthew happy to live with them?

She made tea, and sat.

It was nothing like her parents' house in West London, even though Matthew must be the same generation. That had been a vast detached house in a quiet road not far from the country club where her mother had spent most of her life. Playing tennis, playing bridge, playing. She could remember most of it, the huge sitting room and diningroom, the hall that was decorated at Christmas, the same decorations every year. A centre light, a gothic creation with numerous flame-like bulbs on a circular crown suspended on chains; she wanted to swing from it. Never allowed. There were many evenings when the house glowed with warmth, the kitchen busy, the diningroom laid for twelve and she was banished to her room before any guest could arrive. In earlier years, she had crept out to the landing, peering through the balusters at the arrivals, fur coats taken by the maid, the suffocating smell of face powder, perfume and moth balls. Rarely did a face look up, wondering; and she would vanish backwards, flee to her room. She knew that her parents didn't like to mix children with their social life. They didn't like to mix children with their life at all, actually.

Elizabeth had been shipped off to school at six even though it was wartime, a weekly boarding school that she hated. The silly giggling girls. A late only child, she was always smartly turned out in new clothes, aloof and cold. She had little interest in other children; she didn't know any. Had rarely played with the children of neighbours and hated their noise, their demands, their clothes and toys. Her own life was more powerful; she had her own way with no competition or distractions. At school, she was interested in her schoolwork, not in her classmates. Over the years, she began to notice some variation in the girls around her and recognise that some might be interesting. At later schools, she made a few friends and even stayed with a few of them in the holidays. But would never invite them back to her home.

Her mother was distant and smoked; embarrassing. Elizabeth resisted the rare maternal embrace, usually a display for mother's friends. She had turned her head away from the awful aroma of perfume, lipstick and smoke. That she associated with all adults. She couldn't remember a bedtime kiss or hug. By the time she was fourteen, she shrugged off any attention directed at her; she had taken herself through her first period and buying underwear. Her father, also distant, smiled, hands in pockets. She remembered his smiles, sleek and satisfied like a cat. He had bestowed a generous allowance on her from an early age, a sop to satisfy the guilt they suffered from having a child to whom they gave such a limited attention. An unwanted child, she supposed. A mistake.

Her departures from home, for boarding school, summer camps, and University, were marked by polite suppers that she was required to attend; all her other meals were in the kitchen. Her father would make a speech, read aloud from her school reports, give limited praise for her repeated top marks in all subjects, a little encouragement to make friends – 'you never know when they will be useful' – and a handshake, as though she was a junior partner in his City business. A suggestion that they understood each other. She never knew what the business was, only that it concerned finance. Nothing to do with money in the pocket but stocks and shares, funds and futures, occasionally imports and exports. She couldn't recall seeing him dressed in anything other than a suit. The photographs on the piano included some of his years in the army; he had had a post in England, something to do with Stores. The other photographs, his parents when they met and posing with important friends, bore no resemblance to the parents that she knew.

She had her allies: the maid who came in five times a week and the cook who lived in, a small attic room that Elizabeth was allowed to visit when her parents were out. She knew them well, their homes, families, illnesses, holidays, clothes, smells, tastes. They told her of lives that she could never know, like fairytales, inhabited by names like Fred and Bill, and their strange activities when they came home on leave, 'up the club' or 'down the pub'. And after the war, the factory. Their world, the maid and the cook, was the kitchen, which her mother rarely visited. Elizabeth would sit in her Fair Isle jersey and her tartan kilt on a stool at one side. The cook made little biscuits for her and cakes to take back to school in her tuck box. The maid, widowed in the last years of the war, taught her to sew and mend her own clothes. Elizabeth called her The Crow; it was a term of endearment. She wore round lensed glasses of the type that were popular twenty years later with the likes of John Lennon and Donovan, and a black cardigan with a black scarf over her hair when dusting. She would stand behind Elizabeth on her stool, wrap her arms around her and tell her in great detail about her deceased husband, his habits, his love-making, what he liked, what she liked. The cook would tut-tut, sometimes hush her as a matter of duty, sometimes join in with 'yes, I like that' and so on. The pre-pubescent Elizabeth, not interested in sex or boys, filed the information for future scrutiny. The other information, concerning clubs and pubs, shopping and eating, she found irrelevant and forgot almost immediately.

In later years, she was known for instructing her school colleagues in techniques far beyond their years and boyfriends' ken. The teachers, obtaining a whiff of their illicit education, refused to believe it of the academically brilliant, withdrawn, serious little girl. They blamed an overweight, precociously early developed dullard who went through her school years having no idea of what she was accused, or indeed, what the girls were talking about.

As she grew up, she spent even less time with her parents. Ironically, the adult Elizabeth became an object of interest, invited to dine with them, come to the country club. They were always friendly, glad to see her, ask how her life was going. How long ago it seemed; both of her parents had died in an air crash when she was at Oxford, on a flight to the Caribbean, and her home had disintegrated, cook and maid disappearing, house and contents sold off. All she had were the photographs, pictures of a couple that she never really knew.

Matthew appeared. They ate breakfast. The rain had lifted; a watery sun pressed against the windows. He looked tired as though Edward had sapped his strength. It had been a late night. She asked how he was managing; he looked round the kitchen and gazed out of the window before replying.

'It's strange,' he said. 'So many years spent in company with a wife, children, partners. Life is very quiet now.'

'Why did you move?' she said.

'Why? Oh, I don't know. No, that's not true, I do know. I couldn't bear staying in the old town, always being known as The Widow, always being seen as the one recognised by the wife who had died. Can you see it? I would be invited out to supper, a single man; occasionally, there would be a widow or a divorced woman. Our friends were always very understanding, too understanding. I wanted to step outside that world, to leave all that where I would always be known as Isobel's husband. And we had been coming here for years, ever since the children were young. Just after the war. Daniel and his brother and sisters came Youth Hostelling here after that and Isobel and I came to walk.'

'How does Keswick suit you? You can't be walking all the time.'

'I'm just getting to know it. I'm not a great one for spending evenings in the pub, but there are a couple where I have lunch now and then. They seem to know me. And then there's the café; there is a table of local people and they always insist that I sit with them. It's a good crowd, mostly women. Some divorced, most widowed. But young in spirit. Active. Some want to walk with me; don't you think that I would put them off? Walking in all weathers, high peaks, long days out at height? I don't know. I don't want to put them off.'

'Go for it, Matthew. Nothing to be lost. They're all grown-up; they'll tell you if it too much for them.'

'What about you? I guess that you not a great walker.'

'No, I ...'

Edward appeared. He yawned and sat down, scratching his head. Matthew made toast, offered him a cooked breakfast but he declined. Elizabeth went upstairs. When she came down, she found Matthew sitting by himself, reading the paper.

'Edward has deserted us, I think. Said he was tired, will be bad company, was going to do a little exploring by car. Get to know the area, he said. What would you like to do?' He seemed a little upset.

Bloody Edward, selfish fool. 'I'm so sorry, Matthew. It's very rude of him, particularly after you invited him to walk. He was looking forward to it; I don't know what has got into him. Work has been stressful recently.'

'Well, the weather isn't great. What would you like to do?'

'Anything you like; don't let me be a burden.'

Matthew was looking at her and she wondered what he was thinking. They had only met once before, a weekend a month before.

She smiled. 'I can go into town by myself.'

'Wouldn't hear of it. Come on, I'll be a guide, show you my town, the things I do.'

Elizabeth put her hands up. 'Take me up a hill, if you want. But I would love to see your town, what you do.'

Matthew laughed, looked at the sky. 'I don't think that you are that keen on the hills. Let's go into town, I'd be happy to show you around. How is your London life? I get the impression that life is busy, full of work.'

'Yes, but it's the life we want,' she said. 'I would get so bored if I was shut up at home with children; I need to work, Matthew. Edward is the same; sometimes though, he drives himself too hard.'

'He did seem very withdrawn this morning. Last night, he was chatting away …'

'Oh please, don't worry. We haven't been communicating very well this week, too much work and too many busy evenings. It doesn't do us any good and it gets pretty frustrating, not communicating. I don't know what the problem is but we will be fine, you'll see. But what about you? Don't you get a little lonely, by yourself here?'

He looked surprised; she wondered if she had stepped too far into his private life. Her question came from her own feelings, her own loneliness at home. She was about to apologise, to withdraw, when he began to speak, gazing out of the window as though he was speaking to himself. Had Daniel ever had such a conversation with his own father? She didn't know.

Her knowledge of families was limited, to the failures that came to the Courts, to Edward's and her own backgrounds, very similar.

'I haven't thought about it since Isobel's death. No, that's not true; we were a large busy family. Yes, of course I miss that intimacy, that closeness. I met her at university and we clicked. Before that, grammar school and university life were more sociable; funny that, with a girlfriend things became more confined, less sociable as though we only had time for each other.

'But before Isobel, I had a wild time, coffee bars, going to clubs, listening to early English jazz, dancing with an endless line of girls, all beautiful and dressed the same way, always teasing you. And then after you have been going a while with your girlfriend, when you have done all the things you dared, that it was safe to do in those days, as well as going to the cinema, dancing, drinking – a little, shopping trips, staying with relations, talking about the future, well, it seemed that one had to get married; that was the next thing. Once engaged, well it was different; camping trips, a holiday abroad, walking the Swiss Alps, keeping away from Germany of course. It was just a question of time before you had to settle down. A house in a good neighbourhood. Holidays. Mortgage. Pension plans. With the war butting in, of course.'

Elizabeth thought he sounded depressed, listing inevitabilities as though he had had no choices in life. She had been lucky; she knew that. Saw people every day who had had to follow an inevitable path, to the office or factory, to live, to survive.

'What did you do in the war?'

'I was too old for the normal conscription. I was a gunnery instructor and then they sent me to North Africa. A short time with the Eighth and then a civil administrator. That was terrible, a completely alien culture.'

'What did you do?' Elizabeth was fascinated. She hadn't realised that English lawyers were employed working in other countries during the war, other countries with such different cultures.

'They would bring me two men, one with his hand cut off. The one with his hand cut off had been caught stealing and I was meant to say that that was a very bad thing to do – both the stealing and cutting off the hand. And the man who had caught him stealing, who had cut off the hand, was expecting me to sentence the cripple to death; he had only done what his culture had been doing for oh, some two thousand years. And you think your justice is well established. Mind you, it might have made things simpler for him; the cripple, I mean. He was probably going to died of starvation or gangrene.'

Elizabeth was silent; Matthew looked drawn, lost inside himself. How different his law had been from her work in Chambers and Courts. Daniel had told her that he was a country solicitor, all wills and land purchase and conveyancing. A simple life where the law changed little; not a branch of law that she knew at all.

After a while, he said, 'Sorry, I don't often think of it. Best not. You see what I mean by alien. Come on, we should go out.'

A day of easy companionship. Elizabeth found Matthew's legal past interesting – Matthew couldn't imagine why – and Matthew enjoyed Elizabeth's company. There were people who knew Matthew, if only by sight; she was looked at, and looked back. He enjoyed it, felt good walking beside her. They lunched in a pub and had morning coffee and afternoon tea in his favourite café. On both occasions, there were friends there who greeted him, persuaded them to join their table, asked inquisitive questions of Elizabeth, congratulated Matthew on his company. He gave up describing her husband, her London life and let her say whatever she felt liked. There were a few who suspected that Matthew had found a new partner.

In the pub, they stayed long talking of their pasts.

Elizabeth asked, 'What are you going to do with yourself? Is it walking and painting?'

'That's quite a question. I suppose so; doesn't sound much, does it?'

'Can I tell you about a couple of friends of mine? ... OK. I was thinking of two university friends, both divorced within the last few years. One still lives in her stockbroker house, rattling around and putting up with her children's invasions from time to time, and apparently having no sort of life of her own. I despair of her; what a waste of a life!'

'Isn't she living the life that she wants?'

'She was always such a bright person, interested in so many things, involved with societies and amenity groups. And a good cook. She always told me that when the children were grown up, she would start a business, a small catering firm. But all she does now is clip her roses. We don't even have the same conversations any more and she's not interested in coming to London and having a good time. What does one do?'

'You could try taking her on holiday. It's the best way of taking people out of themselves. What about your other divorced friend?'

'Ah! She is so different. Actually, I get quite envious of her. She was at Somerville with me; a shy, proper little girl, rarely socializing, very untuned to boys. She could be quite good company in college when she had had a little to drink; scandalous stories of people that we knew, sometimes quite famous people. I think her father was something in the Government. And then in third year, she suddenly acquired this boyfriend, quite a bit older than her. He was a junior Fellow at some college. I remember her asking some strange questions one evening; I think that she was still a virgin and wondered what it was like to sleep with a man. Perhaps he was pressing her. I don't remember what I told her; I was quite fortunate to have had a number of lovers at that time and I didn't think that she had anything to worry about. It was so simple in those days; just protection against nasty diseases and pregnancy. Yes, I enjoyed those years. Not so good these days.'

'These days?' he said.

'Well, Edward works very hard and doesn't seem to want my company much. Bit frustrating, actually. It wasn't all smooth running at Oxford. Has Edward told you about our past? 'Spose there was no reason to. Anyway, in those days, he was happier with one night stands, before he met me; didn't want to get tied down. We met at a Union debate, you know. I had heard of his reputation, and I let him pursue me for some weeks before I gave in; we were both attracted to each other, both a bit competitive I'll agree, but he was good company. Anyway, I wasn't going to let him take me over; we both carried on pretty much as before with other partners. My God! How different it is when you are young! After third-year, we went off on holiday together and after the summer, rented a flat in Woodstock Road. Expensive, but we were banking against future earnings. Then I found he was going out with some young undergraduate and we broke up and I moved back into college; jolly lucky to get a room at short notice. I think someone had left. Well, our law courses went on for another two years and we kept bumping up against each other and got married as we left Oxford. You know the kind of thing; wedding in his college chapel, champagne on the lawn, parents and relations put up at the Mitre. And then work; lots of work.'

'You never had children?'

'No,' she said, 'it didn't work out.' She didn't want to say more.

There was a pause and he went off to the bar for more drinks. Elizabeth was sitting with her head down, remembering.

With a burst, she said, 'I was telling you of Angelica. Well, she married her Fellow at some stage and I didn't hear much for some years; they were in the North, some dull University town, producing their family or so I thought. And then I bumped into her about three years ago at an Art Fair in Islington. My God! I didn't recognize her; it was she who grabbed me and told me that I hadn't changed. She was chic, beautifully dressed and looked about ten years younger. She was there representing a Paris gallery. I managed to persuade her to have supper with me and we have become firm friends. Apparently, she had got bored with her Fellow and his job in the North and came into a little money from a deceased aunt. She travelled, did some swatting and managed to transform herself into an art specialist; goodness knows how. After a spell in Cork Street, she went off to Paris and got a very good job in a gallery that deals in twentieth century European art. I can't remember what she read at Oxford but she seems fluent in two or three languages and has acquired a good working knowledge of the art world. I still can't get over the transformation; it must have taken some guts to change one's life like that.'

'Yes, it's difficult, isn't it? There just isn't time to switch about if you're working in a profession and building up the business and contacts. I look back now and the forty years or so of working life seemed condensed into a thick mesh, highlighted by a few very good holidays and particularly successful cases. I suppose that your friend was unfettered with children or a career and that gave her freedom. I was reading the other night of certain well-known actors who wondered whether they were free of career expectations. They had gone on the stage at university, enjoyed it while reading their law degrees or whatever, been offered acting jobs after university and never left. And some of them, you know, didn't know what to do, didn't know whether the acting thing was just temporary and when they were going to pick up that career where it was dropped. And a few of them have gone back to university after they have felt too old and too tired to appear on stage.'

'I can't see myself changing career,' said Elizabeth. 'I am applying for QC shortly and life should get more remunerative and more interesting. Who knows, I may even have more spare time. In which case, I shall certainly spend more time in Paris with Angelica. She has a beautiful flat on the Left Bank and she has introduced me to some wonderful dress shops. She lives a bright sociable life with goodness knows how many lovers and a cat. I can't wait to go back; sorry, Matthew, I won't pretend that I don't prefer continental cities and warm beaches. Why don't you come over? You could put up at a small hotel; I'm sure that Angelica could find one nearby and introduce you to some of her friends.'

Matthew smiled. 'Sounds good. Do you know, I've got out of the habit of going abroad. When I retired, we had great plans, travelling over the world slowly on freight ships, seeing the things that we had only dreamt about. And those dreams evaporated with her death, went out of the window. And I moved here; this is my world and I'm just beginning to know it. The Lakes is a whole world, lowland and highland, farming and coast, town and villages. It's difficult to explain what the hills do.'

'Try me. Please.'

He sat still, staring at the floor. Would he tell her, or was it something private, something to be discovered by every individual for themself? It wouldn't be like Paris: the warm welcome of a boulevard pavement in spring sunshine, a hum of almost sexual excitement, so full of sensual experiences that you had to laugh or groan. Matthew looked at her.

'You could call it a simple benediction; or a place of elemental judgement. Nothing of normal importance matters up there on the hills; you know, the cost of fuel or whether the car needs servicing or a broken cooker that needs replacing. All gone, totally unimportant. It's just you and where you are. And it's different every time – weather, rock, legs, mind – oh yes, mind plays a big part, being able to relax, no, that's not the word, go … yes, go into a different state and commune with it all. Where the only imperative is surviving.'

She could not imagine it. It sounded unnecessarily exposed, like school runs in the rain or rowing practice at dawn on the Thames. He made it sound as if the hills had to be a solo experience; it was all too lonely for her. She hadn't enjoyed school and had had few friends. But there had always been other people around, a crowd that one moved through, sometimes scorning, setting oneself apart but still a crowd.

'Life's better with a partner, isn't it?' she said.

Matthew did not answer. They left, shortly after.

Back at his house, they sat. She felt that they were talked out. After a while, he rose without a word and went out to his studio. It was not a place that she felt comfortable intruding on. She pretended to read and dozed. The afternoon passed.

Edward appeared before supper. He looked tired, unpeeling layers of scarf and coat, dropping them around.

Elizabeth looked at him. 'Had a good day? You were a bit of a pig leaving Matthew like that.'

He did not reply. Avoided her eye, disappeared upstairs. He came down looking more relaxed, a slight smile, hugged Elizabeth briefly, opened wine.

Matthew came in and sat with them. They drank wine and Matthew asked him about his work and wondered when he might see them again, when Edward would like to walk. Edward said that he was very busy; the new owners were cracking the whip. Law had become a commercial enterprise, profit and loss, not much, as far as Edward could see to do with clients. Unless they were wealthy corporations. But Matthew was very welcome to come and stay with them. Elizabeth didn't want to listen to talk of work; she had enough of that at home. It was only when they were away that they seemed to talk of other things, where life was taking them, what they wanted in life. Who they were. She asked Matthew about his home.

'You know,' said Matthew, 'When I was sitting in my old home in Leeds and then in my rented cottage, I thought I would have a house just like the one we had in Leeds. I had never imagined that home would be like this house.'

Elizabeth had been surprised. She had known Daniel for a long time and would never have imagined that there was a spark of modernism in his family's blood. Yes, he did talk about modern American culture but there was none of it at his home. And Mary was so far from her image of an American housewife that … it was laughable. But in Keswick they had arrived at a 1950s house east of the centre of town up the hill a little, looking out towards the lake. The house was pure 1930s modernism, sweeping windows, circular staircase, living spaces running around a great fireplace. Upstairs, a little simpler; privacy and clean lines. Even the bathroom looked as if it came out of the 1930s. Elizabeth thought that it would take a whole water tank to fill the bath.

'I looked around a bit,' said Matthew, 'and couldn't find anywhere with a view. I really wanted a good view and normally you have to pay a king's ransom to get one. And then there was this house. It had been on the market for a year; nobody wanted it. It was empty, belonged to an old lady, a painter's wife. Old fashioned, awkward, needed work, new bathroom and kitchen; still does, come to that. You know the sort of thing. I couldn't understand it when I first saw it. Didn't look like my idea of a house, you know, with a pitched tiled roof, windows with little panes, mouldings round the rooms, four panelled doors. I spent time here, almost a whole day once. Brought a picnic with me and a chair and a book. Moved around with the sun, looked out the windows, lay on the floors even. I couldn't leave it. Bought it.'

'I've been looking at houses,' Edward said. 'There seems to be a moratorium on modern design. It's amazing that this was allowed.'

Elizabeth looked up, suspiciously. What the hell had he been up to now? A house in London that had cost them ... And he wanted more property?

She said, 'Where have you been –'

'I love it, Matthew, the whole area. It seems to be private and open all at the same time. I am really jealous. We've been talking about a house up here and I've had a day looking around. There's some nice houses on the market not far away.'

'We've been talking'? Oh what crap. Elizabeth felt a black wall rising round her, closing in on her, shutting out the future, all hope. She slammed her glass done on the table. Anything to break out ... He carried on as though she wasn't there.

'It's not that we are ungrateful for your hospitality but it would be good to have a base up here where we could introduce some of our friends to the area, but hey, have you over and return your hospitality, spend more time up here in the future.'

She was struggling, fighting to stop the blackness crushing her, a roaring in her ears ... Edward ignored her, carried on.

'I don't know how much houses are up here; it would be an investment, of course. But if we could find an old farmhouse or even a small country house, no cottage of course, we could look at one in any condition. Do you know of any good builders and architects up here? We'd need someone to keep an eye on it for us of course; there must be some housewife who would be glad of a bit of cash, do a bit of cleaning, turn the heating on and so on.'

Matthew looked at Elizabeth, raised his hand, was about to talk.

'And how often do you think we would come up here?' said Elizabeth. Her words dropped like ice cubes, sharp, shattering, creating a void around the two of them, a clear crystalline space in which they were frozen, staring at each other. Matthew had to look away, shocked by the vibrations that resonated between them. Edward was being bloody, riding careless over all, spurs hacking, riding high to victory.

'Well, I don't know. But we could lend it to friends, perhaps even hire it out. What do you think?'

Who was he asking? Matthew or her? She saw in his eyes defiance, evasion and a little fear.

'I don't feel that I belong anywhere,' said Edward. 'That's part of the problem. Not having kids excludes us from so much in London and among our friends. How simple it must have been to inherit a farm and just carry on your father's business among the same people that you were brought up with in the same place.'

'Oh, Edward. I can't think of anything so boring,' said Elizabeth. 'And you would be bored yourself out of your tiny mind; where would you buy shirts? You only get them in Jermyn Street! Really, Edward, are you feeling old this morning? Ready to settle down into senility? Oh, I'm sorry, Matthew, I don't mean that in your case; I think what you are doing is completely right though it wouldn't suit me. But Edward, I can see you going out of your mind stuck in a rural idyll. And what about me? Or don't I come into it?'

Perhaps for the first time, a taste of the parting of ways crept into her mind; she turned it over, rolling it over her tongue. Interesting, had opportunities.

Edward sat in silence. Matthew went out; she heard him making coffee. He must be confused; supper had been forgotten. She frowned at Edward who opened another bottle of wine. Elizabeth stood up, walking round the room, quick impatient steps. The space between them grew, chilled. Matthew came in, offered coffee.

'But supposing, supposing,' Edward said, putting up a hand to halt Elizabeth. 'We had a country house that we might retire to in the fullness of years. And supposing that we bought that house now while we have the means and energy to do it up, we would have the opportunity to get to know the area a little, to know people and tradesmen. When we visit, we are not tourists but accepted and later we settle into the area as known residents, not brash Londoners who have decided to buy into a beauty spot and find that they don't like it. And if it didn't work out, we could still sell and try elsewhere.'

Elizabeth thought of Paris, of light and colour and music. And warm company and sex. She wondered, briefly, how it balanced with a life up here with Edward; the weather, all those cold hills, those dreadful walking shops with 'practical' clothes, loneliness. She felt the blood rise and pressed her hands against her cheeks. She was unable to contain herself, spitting out her words.

'Is that what you want, Edward? Is that what I've worked for for all these bloody years? To be buried in a country idyll with you when I'm not slaving away in the Courts or Chambers? I don't get it; I don't know you. You know bloody well that I like to get away, to escape all the toil and the weather and the English people and escape; yes, escape from everything. And why not? And now you want to play squire and take on more commitment and in this fucking climate.'

Edward looked surprised. 'But Elizabeth –'

She was standing, arms raised, staring at him.

'Yes, I know, it's a very good boring idea and in twenty years I'll be sorry that we haven't done anything and live to regret it for ever and we don't have children to look after us in our old age and it's all going to go terribly wrong. God!' she said with disgust, 'you're starting to sound like those advertisements for pensions that used to be fired at us when we were in our twenties; the ones when the faces gradually get wrinkled and the words go from 'perhaps we ought to start a pension' to 'why didn't we start a pension when we were younger'. Well, I'm not going to live for my old age; it's just going to have to creep up on me as it likes; I'm going to live a full enjoyable life because I shan't be young for ever and I work for it and I'll bloody well do it without you if I have to.'

And vanished upstairs.

Edward looked embarrassed for about two minutes, staring out of the window. Elizabeth came back after a while, her face closed, meeting no-one's eyes and accepted coffee.

'I want to go home. Now. Go and get your things, I've packed.'

He stared.

'Get a bloody move-on. If you won't, I'll call a taxi.'

He disappeared upstairs. Elizabeth hugged Matthew; she was shaking, weeping.

'I'm sorry, very sorry, Matthew. You don't deserve it, it's not fair to you. We must go, leave you in peace. Come and see us in London. Do. And thankyou, thankyou for the day in town, I enjoyed it so much.'

Elizabeth wondered who was going to drive; Edward had drunk at least half a bottle of wine. She was buggered if she was going to, he would have to manage. She could always stick a pin in him if he looked like not concentrating.

They left, Matthew looking after them.

CHAPTER 4

April

The children had gone off to school with little fuss; Mari had a mock GCSE exam, maths she thought, and seemed to have no worries at all. She hadn't told them about it and Mary hadn't been aware that she had done any revision. Perhaps a good failure would teach her a lesson. The boys were looking forward to athletics; they were practising for an inter-school match at a sports centre. She looked round the house, picked up a few clothes and toys, and decided to leave the rest. It was a warm sunny day in April, too good to waste on housework. Or repairing the rainwater pipe by the door. She found herself looking round for something to do, something to fill the time. Was it possible to get back into nursing? She had no idea. Sort it out some other day. It would be quite good to have a job, have some sort of role in the world, some significance. She felt side-lined by her husband and her children who were busy all the time. What sort of job could she do? The check-out girls at supermarkets looked as bored as hell; that wouldn't do. She couldn't type or speak any foreign languages or sew or cut wood or mend machinery. She didn't feel very suited to the job market; all she had was an outdated nursing qualification, one that wouldn't get her into any hospital. But perhaps some clinic, working under a better qualified nurse half her age – she shivered.

Even her writing was difficult. She was stuck with the story; she couldn't go on as before, sex scene after sex scene. There had to be some story to it, some trouble perhaps, something to hang all the rest on. But she didn't know about writing, didn't know about plot development and characters and tense and all those things that she had heard people talking about on the radio. And she had no idea how to get into that; it never occurred to her to do a creative writing course, or even buy a book on writing. Didn't think she needed them; she wasn't an intellectual. She had assumed that it came naturally; you just sat down and typed away or scribbled, whatever.

She opened her wardrobe and started pulling out her clothes onto the bed. They seemed tired and worn, she hated them. She went faster and faster until the wardrobe was empty, apart from a winter coat, her only long evening dress and shoes scattered at the bottom. Rushing downstairs, she brought up two bin bags and started to stuff clothes into them, hardly looking at what she was doing. After a few minutes, she tore off the clothes she was wearing, sat down on the bed in her bra and knickers and wept, hugging her arms about her.

The telephone rang, eight rings, and stopped.

A blackbird called, a sharp alarm.

She lifted her head and looked out of the open window. It was quiet, the distant roar of traffic dulled. A rose bush, trained against the wall, gave off a strong sweet scent. A sparrow landed on the cill and stared at her. She got up and went to the window, watching the sparrow flutter down to the lilac bush by the gate. And became aware of a delivery driver looking up at her.

She retreated from the window, covering herself with her arms. Really, she thought, this won't do. Emptying the bin bags, she spread the clothes out on the bed, returned a few to the bags and spent some time selecting clothes for the day. A tight skirt, just long enough; she hadn't worn it for years. Thank goodness the fashions these days allowed her to wear what she chose. A shirt that matched the skirt. That was better. Now, shoes, better underwear, a little jewellery and some slap. She felt happier and turned in front of the mirror, a faint smile on her face, and brushed her hair vigorously. She turned on the radio, made face at the music and turned it off.

Going downstairs, she imagined herself as a visitor, ignoring the worn decorations, the discarded shoes, coats tumbling off the hooks in the hall and junk mail piled on the window cill. The house was another Daniel, scattered belongings and obligations – the children in it, in him – but she was not. In the kitchen, she chose one of the best cups and saucers, made coffee and took it into the sittingroom where she sat, sipping in silence, perched on the edge of an armchair. She glanced at her watch. What should she do now? Go shopping for something that she couldn't afford and still be alone? Company, she craved company. Where else?

The university was approaching the end of the morning. The grass was mown, tight and smooth. The blossom from the cherry trees had scattered a cheery polka dot pattern on the paths. Students sat in the sun, drinking coffee, chatting and laughing, walking, sometimes arm in arm. Lovers stretched out on the ground with books, murmuring. It seemed clean and well-ordered as if everything was in its place; no shouting, loud music or unpleasantness. She sat on the nearest bench and then decided to move near Daniel's office; he could take her out to lunch. Why not? The senior common room dining was not too bad, away from students and junior staff. They could talk of this and that, where they might take holidays, whether he thought she was dressed well, whether he should have some new clothes. She went over to his department and sat on a bench with some students. They made room for her politely and shortly left her alone. She glanced at her watch; lunchtime. She felt hungry.

A bird paused on the end of her bench, its head on one side.

The doors swung open and a crowd of students poured out, overflowing onto the grass laughing, talking loudly in short sentences, bright clothes, bare arms, some touching their friends, a few hugs, one couple kissing. The crowd thinned and she watched the doors. Daniel emerged, arms rigidly at his sides, hands fidgetting in his pockets, head down, talking to a young blonde girl who skipped alongside, books clutched to her chest. Mary raised her arm, unable to interrupt the flow of conversation. He stopped, his back to her, took a piece of paper from his pocket and a pencil and scribbled. The girl took it, smiled, thanked him and chased after the crowd. He hummed to himself and walked off down the path. Mary stood and called. Daniel disappeared.

There was no heat in the sun. The blossom was a brazen pink, the polka dot pattern pathetic, the grass a harsh green. The young people looked brash in vulgar clothes, too eager, no doubt soon to be disappointed in life. She turned and walked slowly away.

Mari came home early. She found her mother sitting in the kitchen, doing nothing. Her face looked wan, tired. Mari didn't say anything but made a pot of tea, opened a new packet of biscuits and sat down.

The house was silent.

She poured two mugs of tea and looked at her mother.

'Would you like to go shopping? I really need something for Rachel's party.'

Her mother looked at her as if noticing her for the first time and sipped her tea. 'Would you like to?' she asked. 'Usually, you don't want to go with me.'

Mari looked at her. Something was not right with her mother. Mari looked confused for a moment, a little frightened, and then something resolved in her.

'Come on,' she said. 'The boys won't be home for ages; let's go into town.'

Mary allowed herself to be led out of the house up the road to the bus stop and have a ticket bought for her. In town, Mari took charge and it was good. She watched her daughter, noted how assured she was, confident with sales people, sensible in her choice of clothes. She felt proud, with a tinge of regret; how fast she was growing up.

They met a schoolfriend; Mari paused, 'Hi Jaqui, the exam was a stinker wasn't it? This is my Mum. Mum, Jaqui. We're shopping for Rachel's party. See you tomorrow.'

And passed on. The friend stared and was lost in the shoppers.

At home, Mari retreated to her room as usual. Mary sat in the kitchen, waiting for the boys. She couldn't face supper, cooking or eating. She went to the telephone and called Elizabeth's Chambers. A polite secretary told her that Elizabeth was at Court but that she would be happy to take a message. Mary rang off; she wished that they could communicate privately by mobile 'phone. Although Elizabeth had one, an expensive brick-like thing that she only used in London, Mary didn't own one. She knew nobody in Reading who owned one. Going upstairs, she wrote a card, put on a First Class stamp, and calling to Mari to watch out for the boys, went out to the post box. It made her feel happier. She came home, planning supper, greeted the boys, listened to their tales of success and failure, smiled, sent them off to do homework and prepared supper.

Daniel appeared at suppertime, an over-flowing case in his arms, a weary smile. Mary waited until the children had finished and gone, and sat looking at him.

'Have you had a good day?'

Daniel looked surprised; it wasn't often that she asked.

'Yeah, ok. Bit warm, don't you think?'

'What did you do for lunch?'

'Lunch? I don't know. Stayed in my office. I think.'

'Really?'

Daniel looked up at her tone, now sharp. He appeared to be re-evaluating the situation, trying to determine what it was that he had missed. He looked at her clothes.

'I can't remember. Maybe I went to the canteen. You're dressed up; have you been out?'

'I was there.'

'There?'

'Yes.'

'Where?'

'Outside your department.'

'I never saw you.'

'No.'

'Why didn't you come to me?'

'I called. And waved.'

'What?'

'You spoke to a student, a young blonde one, and then walked off. I called, you just walked off.'

'Oh yes, June. She wanted a –'

'You just walked off. And you didn't see me. Sitting on the bench by your door.'

'I'm sorry, I guess I was thinking –'

'You're always thinking of something or other. And now you don't notice anything. Not even me.'

'What –'

'You don't notice me, do you?'

'What do you mean? Of course, I –'

'No, you don't. You didn't see what I was wearing when you came in.'

'You're looking very nice –'

'You didn't notice. I could be dressed in bin bags, with a plaster on my face, and you wouldn't notice.'

'Of course I would. Don't be silly. I –'

'I thought that you might take me out to lunch.'

'I would love to have –'

'You have never suggested it. Never. As if I didn't exist, when you are at the university.'

'But love, –'
'You clear the dishes. I'm going out.'
'Out?'
'Yes, I want company.'
'Would you like me to come?'
'You don't have time, do you?'
'Well –'
'I thought so. See you later.'
'No, I'll make time. I'll come –'
'No, I'm going alone. You can look after everything here.'

She walked out of the house, down the road, careful not to look back. At the end of the road, she realised that she had no money, no keys, and it was getting cooler. She walked around for an hour getting cold, wondering whether she could drop in on friends but deciding that they might think that she was off her rocker. She went home. There she ignored everybody and crawled into bed, her head beneath the bedclothes, shivering. Daniel found her later and gently removed her shoes, tucking the blankets around her.

Two days later, she was on the train to London. The same skirt, the same shirt and underwear. This time, there would be company. She had told Daniel that she needed time out, a break from the daily dirge, and she had arranged to meet Elizabeth in London to look at pictures and go out to lunch. Daniel had welcomed the idea initially but looked worried. She could see that he dared not mention either the cost or the length of time that she would be away; he would have to change his schedules, come home early, prepare supper for the children and see them to bed. While Mary had a day off, a day free of all the normal cares, free of her family and husband.

Elizabeth was waiting for her in Mayfair at a small gallery where they looked at photographs of naked women and men, Imogen Cunningham, Steichen, Man Ray and others. These were black and white images in wide glossy black frames, precise, detailed and remote.

She took her to lunch in a little café nearby. Mary wondered how Elizabeth knew London so well; it always seemed like a jungle where she kept to well trodden paths beaten down over years and rarely went off path. Over lunch, Elizabeth was business-like, wasting no time; after a few preliminary questions, she laid down a simple proposal – the ground rules, the possibilities, the benefits. Mary listened, one part of her not believing what she was hearing, another gulping in the details with a ready greed, wanting more. She thought of her own writing and how it missed the realities, the nub of the matter. Proverbs randomly came to her – 'no time like the present', 'striking while the iron is hot'; all inadequate. She blushed, restrained a giggle. They taxied to Bond Street, a little boutique where Elizabeth was greeted like an old friend and offered a new range of French underwear. Elizabeth laughed. Mary froze, a sudden panic, wide-eyed, before Elizabeth took her arm, lead her into a cosy changing-room.

Mary tried on gorgeous underwear, item after item. She was embarrassed at Elizabeth's largesse, unable to refuse any of it. I'll pay you back, she thought. One day. Embarrassed at being paraded in a private room, dressed so scantily. But the staff were so encouraging, so nice, so appreciative. And Elizabeth watched over her, watching the transformation. She didn't care what she was being transformed into, she felt like a schoolgirl with a rich aunt. Elizabeth would suggest this, and that, and eventually expressed herself satisfied. Mary insisted on wearing the new underwear immediately. They left the shop; nothing was real any more. Even the weather was perfect and the street full of beautiful people, mostly young and female, beautifully dressed. Reluctantly did she get into a taxi, immediately did she forget the shop and the street.

The hotel off Sussex Gardens was not large, but quiet and luxurious. A marble floor, mahogany counter, deep armchairs, soft carpets, flowers, crisp uniforms. Polish, shine, colour, all a blur; Mary was floating, hardly aware of the taxi journey, the hotel reception, the stairs to the bedroom door.

In the room, she stopped and laughed in a sudden release of tension, staring around her, her bags falling to the floor. The walls and curtains whispered of concealments and private dramas, daring and sometimes dangerous. She felt excited, frightened, nervous. There was a gentle rumble of traffic and the afternoon sun lit the bed and floor. Someone passed in the corridor, possibly a maid with a trolley. She felt the deep carpet and kicked off her shoes. She felt slightly sick, sweaty palms.

'Oh, I don't know …'

Everything, all walls, noises, and fears slowly fell away; she and Elizabeth were standing on a hilltop with nothing else around. Elizabeth was looking at her, a curious expression as though she was holding something back; she started to take off her own clothes, the silence marked by a zip, a jacket falling, skirt, shirt … Mary was slow to respond, breathless, a deafening heart-beat, caught in back time.

Elizabeth stood in bra and knickers. Mary fumbled with buttons, twisted to throw off a jacket and blouse, stood in bra and knickers, hair over her face, breathing deeply. She tossed her head, brushing the hair out of her eyes.

Elizabeth looked at her, smiled and came close, kissing, undoing, revealing, opening, coaxing until Mary was there … there where she was lying on the bed, floating on an unimaginable high; a feeling so foreign, so strange and so comforting; never could she remember such a feeling with her own husband or any boyfriend in the past. Yes, it was right to be with one who could make her feel like this.

Elizabeth laughed, delighted. 'My turn now.'

And Mary lay over her, stroking until the game

became more intense and Elizabeth gave a quiet moue of satisfaction.

They looked at each other; Mary wondered what Elizabeth was thinking. 'Was that all right?' she said.

Elizabeth smiled, licked Mary's shoulder, pulled her down.

Later, Elizabeth went into the bathroom and turned on the taps.

They bathed together, one at either end of the bath. Mary had forgotten that it could feel so good, to be washed and touched all over. Like first love; yes, that is what it was, first love. She was passive, happy to let Elizabeth dictate the pace but as she became excited, her responses overcame her. Elizabeth saw a different Mary rise from the bath, shucking off the old, a Mary she didn't know. This was a Mary who was learning what Elizabeth liked and dared to ask for what she wanted, even demand.

They dried each other with the closest care, stroking, massaging and would have collapsed onto the bed; Mary was willing but Elizabeth smiled and dressed her, starting with the new underwear. Mary felt exhausted, the physical effort and the new sensations left her feeling raw, exposed.

They drank tea.

The Tate was open, a late showing of Van Gogh. They strolled slowly, sometimes their fingers intertwined, letting time and space pass through them as they were entertained by the paintings; the despair and the bleakness of the Flemish scenes passed them by; they saw only colour and bodies, intentions and dreams. They went to the restaurant and ate slowly, a light fish dish, lemon and cream, steamed courgette, a crème caramel to follow. They talked of this and that, clothes, places to visit in London, but never of husbands or children, homes or work.

And bid farewell on the steps, Elizabeth putting Mary into a taxi to catch a train home.

CHAPTER 5

Letters

Reading,
March 1990

Dear Matthew,

We had a lovely weekend with you in the Lakes last weekend. I hope that we weren't too much of a crowd; Daniel was very keen to see Edward and introduce him to you. They enjoy each other's company a lot. I just hope that they weren't rude and cut you out. I often get cut out of the conversation – I don't have any idea what they are talking about.

I hope that you enjoyed meeting Elizabeth. I don't know whether you had a chance to talk to her. She is very bright; I find her a bit intimidating. She is Mari's godmother – did you know? She has no children and I think that she has ideas of leading her astray when she is older. Lucky Mari! It will be a breath of fresh air, a break from home and younger brothers. I'm not sure that I encourage Mari enough in being grown-up, being apart from her brothers. It is so easy to lump them together, and I know it is not really fair; the boys are quite a bit younger, and well, boys! And she doesn't live their life at all, not even much at home. I ought to help her more, encourage her to think and go out and ... But ... she is very difficult. It's almost as if I've missed the boat. She is almost secretive, I have no idea what she is thinking, or where she is. Most of the time. Perhaps it will be a good thing, when Elizabeth takes her under her wing. Perhaps a mother is not the best person to be a friend. Or at least, I'm not the best person. The boys – well, they're easy, like dogs. At least that's what Daniel calls them, his dogs. On the rare occasions that he has to take them to meetings, he always asks if he can bring his dogs and I gather they are always a bit surprised to see two boys!

Daniel is back at work, of course. I see him for a little time morning and evening as he piles up books and folders and goes off to see local politicos or students. It was wonderful to have a weekend away and spend some time with him. Even if he did spend most time sleeping or arguing, I mean discussing with

Edward. Anyway, he says please could I give his love and he will be in touch. I'll bully him to do that, don't worry.

It would be wonderful to come up and see you before too long. I shall speak to Daniel. And bring the children. You may have some good company walking on the hills with the boys. And maybe even Mari. Daniel and I are not very good at it, I'm afraid. But the boys talk about it, ever since last summer. They are hoping that you will take them to the highest peak and the longest walk. Don't worry, I don't think they could manage those.

Do look after yourself. Do you have friend in Keswick yet? I think you mentioned a café where you meet people. Well, I hope there are some interesting people there.

Love to you,
Mary

Islington,
March 1990

Dear Daniel,

Thanks for a terrific weekend in the Lakes. It was really kind of you to introduce us to your father – yes, I know, we met at Oxford. But that's a long time ago and I didn't ever get to know him then.

I'm sorry that you are not more enthusiastic

about walking. I loved the hills, great to get away and above everything, whatever the weather. Wouldn't mind having a little house up there, somewhere to use as a base. You could use it too if you didn't want to burden your father.

Sorry that you can't get excited about Bush. Ok, he is not the brightest but he seems to be pretty much par for the course for American Presidents. And you never know, he might turn out to be a saviour for the free world with people like Sadam around. Do you know, even Tricky Dicky is getting a better press these days. But you would know more about that.

See you soon and take more exercise, you old ...

Yours forever,
Edward

Islington,
March 1990

Dear Matthew,

I am writing for Elizabeth and myself to thank you for putting us up last weekend. It was very enjoyable and so nice to get to know you after such brief meetings in Oxford. Those days seem a long time ago. I was sorry to hear about the loss of your wife; I hope that your new life is fulfilling.

Your introduction to the hills has inspired me. I loved the sense of release and freedom that one experienced up there and I'm particularly grateful to you for that. I wish Daniel were more inspired; he has told me how he used to youth hostel in the Lakes and elsewhere with his brother and sisters. And how they used to protect the youngest sister from over-friendly boys; I gather she wasn't always grateful for their protection. I haven't met them since Oxford days; I hope they are all well and see you in Keswick.

I guess that you used to walk them all on the hills when they were young. Daniel and Mary are not so keen now; pity. I shall have to coax him out of his sedentary ways and encourage him to walk more. Perhaps it might work if I booked us on a guided week's walk in Italy – plenty of exercise to use up the wine and food.

I hope we see you soon. Would you like to come and stay in London? We have a lot of room and are not far from the City. It's very convenient and you would be very welcome, if you wished to revisit your London haunts. Bring somebody with you if you like.

Yours sincerely,
Edward

Keswick
April 1990

Dear Edward,

Thankyou very much for the nights in London; please pass on my thanks to Elizabeth and tell her how sorry I was not to see more of her.

Gosh, how London has changed. I used to get down there quite a bit when I was younger. We used to stay with friends and go to the theatre. I always loved a bit of Shakespeare. I don't remember taking the children with us; it may have been before they were around.

I am very sorry to hear of your doubts and fears in your marriage. I can only repeat my advice – talk, talk, talk. It is the lack of communication that kills things off and we are all guilty of it at times. It is too easy when work seems to take the major player in a marriage. I was lucky, I guess, in that my wife only worked part-time and was always there for the children and for me. I guess that she would have loved to get away more but she always seemed happy in her life.

Do come up and walk; I should be happy to have your company as long as you can limit your energies to allow for an old man. And bring Elizabeth too; even if she doesn't walk, I expect there would be things that she enjoys. I look forward to hearing from you.

Yours,
Matthew.

Islington,
May 1990

Dear Matthew,

What a fantastic weekend. I loved it. Super walking and what an introduction to the area above Wastewater. I never dreamt that one could be so remote and walking at height in England. I loved it.

I'm sorry that Elizabeth didn't come with me. I'm afraid that we haven't been communicating very well and she isn't around very much. I fear that what I told you is happening again; well, maybe it is something that she has to work out of her system. I hope that this doesn't shock you. Anyway, I can't let it get in the way of work.

Work is pretty demanding. Our American bosses seem to think the law business is like any other with time and motion studies and all the rest. Well, not quite time and motion but a close watch on our time. I can't get used to it; there's a groundswell of discontent but I don't think the others will say anything. Just grin and bear it. The salaries are so tempting that they just buckle under it and think of their mortgages and their high spending wives. Let alone the private school fees. Well, I'm considering saying something about it; we have been losing some of our older clients and it is time that something was said. Even if it upsets the other chaps in the firm.

I haven't seen Daniel for a while. I hope they are all well.

Yours, with gratitude,
Edward

Islington
June 1990

Dear Matthew,
I have to write to you to unburden myself and to put you in the picture. I would hate for our friendship to be wrecked and I wish to put my side of things.

As I suggested to you, I was pretty sure that Elizabeth is having an affair; I hardly see her, she is strangely satisfied and distant and all she says is that work is very demanding. It's demanding for both of us but at least I'm home most evenings by seven and she often doesn't appear until bed-time.

The other evening, I was looking for something and I came upon a train ticket, unused, to Reading in her pocket. I know she has no work in Reading; she told me when I slid a question in. She denied knowledge of the ticket and said that it was obviously a mistake at work.

I don't think so. She is obviously having an affair in Reading and there is only one man she knows there – Daniel. She has known him a long time, they have always got on well. But I am deeply shocked that she chooses my oldest friend and I have to speak to him to clear things up and ask him what the hell he thinks he is doing with my wife.

I'm sorry to burden you with this; I didn't want you to get the wrong picture from Daniel. Or Mary.

With best wishes,
Edward.

Keswick,
June 1990

Edward,

I am sorry to receive your letter; I'm not sure that it was appropriate to involve me and I wish that you would reconsider.

Frankly, I think it most unlikely that Daniel is having an affair. I would not dream of asking him; he has to live his own life without my intrusion but he has always been devoted to his family and wouldn't put them at risk.

I fear that you have not taken my advice and spoken with Elizabeth. I'm sure that you can both clear this up with a little communication. Please make the effort.

Yours sincerely,
Matthew

Islington,
July 1990

Dear Daniel,

I have been forced to such an odd conclusion that I need to talk to you. Soon. I don't wish to say more now. Will you be at the University on Tuesday afternoon to spare me a few minutes for a chat? Let me know if you won't be there.

Yours,

Edward

Islington,
July 1990

Daniel,

I don't understand you. I have known you for so many years and now you can't even be straight with me. You wonder why I walked off without saying goodbye.

Do you realise that I took a whole day of work to come down and see you. And ask you to leave Elizabeth alone. And all you can do is pat your stomach, ask who would be attracted to that and laugh in my face. And when I asked you directly whether you were having an affair, you laughed again and said 'For goodness sake, Edward, what is going on?' And you don't know??!!??

Of course, I can't see what Elizabeth sees in you, you fat bastard, and you owe me for a few cases of my wine that you have drunk. I wish I'd punched your fat face and extracted the truth from you. Bring back the rack. We might start getting the truth out of some of the unfortunates that we have to deal with in my line of work. And out of you.

Well, I'm saying good-bye now. Don't ever darken my door, drain my wine, talk to my wife, or greet me ever again.

Fuck off.

Edward

Reading
July 1990

My love ..

I don't know what is going on. Daniel came home yesterday in a strange mood, angry and sullen. He didn't want to talk about it. It was HOURS until I could get a word out of him. Bedtime, actually, just as I was falling asleep remembering how you ...

He said that he had seen Edward that afternoon at the University. I said that was strange. I couldn't remember Edward ever coming to the university. Nothing there to interest him. He said Edward accused him of having an affair with you!!! I didn't say anything. Just wanted to see whether he would say any more. He didn't.

Then this morning, he said that he didn't think that Edward and Elizabeth were our friends anymore. He said that he had been thinking about it all night and couldn't understand why Edward had picked on him.

Couldn't you, would it be possible, just tell him that he has got the wrong end of the broomstick or whatever the saying is? That you are not having an affair, particularly with Daniel? I mean it's not as if we are a threat to either of them. Boys being stupid. If we choose to have a good time together, why should it worry them?

Anyway, I hope they clear it all up soon. Daniel is like a dog in a manger, not talking to us at all, out all hours, untidier than ever before. The children don't really notice, but I hate the atmosphere. Honestly, if only they could just get on with their lives!!

See you next Tuesday, my lover. Until then, I shall dream of ... this and that.

Mary

Islington
July 1990

Mary, my love,

Spoken to Edward. Silly ass. I told him that I spent some time with female company from Chambers – he didn't believe me. I do wonder how long our marriage can go on. It's nothing to do with us – he is so hopeless, and wants different things from me, not at all the type of husband I had once wished for.

Did you know that he wants to buy a house in the Lakes? I told him I wasn't going to be a walking hausfrau but he said it would be a good base for all our friends, a holiday house. I think that there is more to it.

Anyway, next Tuesday. Don't forget your stuff.

Elizabeth.

Reading,
July 1990

Dear Gramps,

I know, you don't like that, but I think it's funny and I used to have a book with a large family, all scruffy with animals and cats and things, and they called their Mum's father Gramps and he was very much loved and a major part of the book.

Anyway, we had a lovely time in the Lakes, apart from the rain, which was quite boring and cold. I particularly liked the day we spent with you while Mum and Dad went off somewhere and we went into the town and you bought us lunch in that lovely café and your friends came up and asked you if you had kidnapped three children. I didn't mean to get huffy at being called a child – SORRY. I didn't really mind – people keep lumping me in with the boys and they're just young, aren't they? I don't have much in common with them, really. Do you think I will ever?

Anyway, the holidays are very boring and we aren't going anywhere or doing anything interesting at the moment. My friend Rachel is going to France with her parents and Daddy is doing a summer school somewhere and Mummy keeps disappearing to London to look at pictures and doesn't want to take us. When do you think that we three could come and stay with you without Mum and Dad? It would be GREAT, even if I do have to look after the bros on the train. I love your house and your friends seemed to be really nice. Perhaps I could have a summer job working at the café and stay with you and cook your meals and things. That would be so cool. As long as the boys aren't there.

I hope that you are well. The boys say Thankyou too but I told them that they ought to write their own Thankyou letters. Daddy had a friend who called them 'roofers', you know, staying under a friend's roof. I guess you might get a note in a Christmas card; one day.

You know that book on Lakes history you showed me? I went to the library to look for other books on the Lakes; there wasn't very much but I'm reading a book about Wordsworth and the Romantics. It's really interesting, all about the Victorians and travel and the first tourists. As well as DAFFODILS. And his poetry. I've never been any good at Poetry; they make us learn boring stuff at school. But I like History, particularly when we learn about ordinary people. We've been learning about the Industrial Revolution and the effect on working people. It's amazing that the population increased with all the disease and accidents in the industrial towns. And I remember what you told me about the tin and silver mining in the Lake. I'd love to walk up and see those places with you. Are there any mines that one can go into? It must have been really hard, walking up the hills before a day's work and then walking all the way down.

I guess I better not use up all of Dad's printing paper. I hope you don't mind a printed letter; I'm learning to type faster for my exams and university essays. Dad says I should go to his College and that all essays have to be typed. So I might as well start typing now. I should be at University in four years and, although that's quite a long time, I shall need typing for A- level essays anyway.

    Lots of love, your loving grand-daughter,
    Mari

p.s I do know that Thankyou letters ought to be hand-written

CHAPTER 6

July

At half past eleven, they arrived and ushered a blast of wet cold air into the house. Matthew closed the door behind them and stood back as boots, anoraks and hats were cast off in a sprinkle of cold water. The cat fled. How strained Daniel and Mary looked, he thought. There they were snapping at their children, who are standing quietly, no trouble to anyone. Mari, a young teenager I see, staring out in a faintly hostile manner from beneath her mass of unruly hair; but what a wonderful colour; is that what they call Rubens Red? She looks like her father. Not that she would appreciate it. She acts as though she was responsible for her brothers, chivvying them into line; she didn't need to do that. The boys: Seb and Josh wasn't it? They're not put out in the least bit, grinning without shyness and looked about them with curiosity. Of course, they haven't been here for a long time. The older one, Seb, looks like his mother, that keeness in face and slender build. His younger brother, Josh, is more like his father, stouter, broad but not fat. Can't say the same for Daniel; he ought to do something about that.

He ignored Daniel and Mary, asked the children what they would like to drink and took them round the house, his books, boat models and collection of shepherds crooks. He left Mari curled up near the CD player and introduce the boys to books on ships and mountaineering, allowing them to pull them out of the shelves. He laughed as they competed in showing each other new discoveries. Mary hovered, an anxious look.

'Come on, Mary, leave them. They're fine, no problem, and I'm delighted to see them exploring my stuff. No; don't clear up after them. They will do that when they are finished, don't you worry.' He took her arm and led her away. The cat looked down from the landing and descended to sit on Mari's lap.

They sat down at the diningroom table and drank coffee. The glazed doors were open to the yard; it sparkled with colour: blue, ochre and sienna from the walls and damp paving, warmed by a watery sun, a buzz of bright colours from the flowers whose smell filled the air. A bee zoomed by casually before descending into a cup of clematis. After the usual polite remarks – Mary had brought cakes – silence came over them as though their senses were dulled by the display.

Time passed. A bird hovered, the wing beats as

distinct as a metronome. In the stillness Matthew found himself back in his painting, lost in the dynamics of his family whose images continued to fade and shift like a collection of broken glass slides. He watched them as though through a window, saw them lean back and appear to relax a little; Mary had, at last, given up watching out for her children but had given Daniel a sharp glance. Who ignored her and settled into a brown muse; he looked exhausted, faded, the flesh falling in like an old mac. His shoulders dropped and he gazed at the floor; Matthew thought he might drop off to sleep. What is becoming of him? I don't remember feeling that bad when working. A butterfly appeared briefly, fluttering over a blossom. Mary took a gulp of coffee, spluttered and looked embarrassed, tracing circles in a splash of spill.

'You can't imagine what it has been like,' she said. 'We only have a single tent and they have nowhere to let off steam when it's raining.'

'Poor Mari, she could do with getting away from the boys for a while,' said Daniel. 'You ought to –'

Mary was sharp, as though by habit.

'And what is she going to do in Keswick on her own? Find some helpful local lad to introduce her to the delights of the town? You know how she is dying to get out at night and still far too young!'

Poor Daniel. He looked stunned at her outburst, shrinking into his mug. Matthew wondered whether he was irresponsible, rarely engaged with his children.

Or whether she was being unfair, frustrated by a holiday that was not a holiday. He suggested that they all go to the Pencil Museum after lunch. Daniel sat up and gave him a big smile. 'That's a great idea, Dad.'

But then Mary asked if she could go to the shops; she said she wanted to get presents for the people at home. Oh well.

'I'll take the boys to the Museum, dear,' said Daniel. 'Are you going alone or will you take Mari?'

Matthew laughed. 'I've never seen the Museum; you know, if you live in a place –'

'Oh, but Matthew,' said Mary, 'I was hoping that you would show me around. I just need a break from the children! Is that alright, darling?' She appealed to her husband, reaching out to him.

Lunch was enjoyable, noisy and boisterous. Matthew entertained the children, telling them tales of the Lakes, describing the farmers and animals; he sensed that he would hear of the parents' problems before long and ignored them. The boys were full of conversation and good humour, inquisitive, interested and polite, occasionally sparring with each other. Only Mari seemed a little reserved and picked at her food. Daniel relaxed, watching the boys with amusement as they attempted to find out the limit of Matthew's experiences on the peaks. Had he been to the highest? How fast could he climb? Was he ever frightened – this from Mari. He suspected that tales of his walking had been exaggerated as though he were an Alpine pioneer;

what a joke. He just loved to be up on the hills but the boys wouldn't understand that yet. He laughed loudly, promised to show them maps, photographs and his compass which he said he had inherited from an African explorer. Not picked up in a charity shop.

Mary was quiet, self-absorbed and indifferent to her daughter's looks of concern. And after lunch, she was impatient to leave the others; Matthew gave Daniel directions while she stood in the yard. The boys were happy, made some caustic comments about their sister, and raced around the house until it was time to leave. Glad to see the back of her family, Mari returned to the music and the cat; their mutual indifference had been cancelled out and each found company in the other.

The rain lifted as they walked into the town. Mary was silent as Matthew pointed out his favourite shops and told tales about the residents. There were a large number of tourists taking shelter; he knew that the pubs and shops would be glad of the trade. Sometimes they wished for rain. On the whole, he thought that there was enough bad weather to maintain business throughout the year; and longer. Mary took little notice of his comments as though he was intruding on her privacy.

When they were in the town centre, she surprised him, 'Could we sit in a coffee shop for a while? It's a bit wet and I could do with a rest.'

They had been sitting over lunch for a couple of hours but he humoured her and led her to the Wild

Strawberry. He liked the slate tables, the stone flagged floor and ancient timbers. The staff greeted him warmly, casting glances at Mary; he could imagine the gossip in the kitchen. Sometimes, he felt that he was approaching an arranged marriage in this town; they could not bear to see an eligible widower going to waste, whatever the age. He laughed with them, accepted a piece of the best cake, and ushered Mary upstairs, away from the bustle and prying eyes. Fortunately, the place was half full and none of his local friends were there. Silence fell, interrupted by the chatter from other tables. Coffee arrived.

Matthew looked at her, waiting for her to speak. His mind wandered away from the café to the hills. Would High Street be busy? And Blencathra, a mystical presence, he must get up there soon. That mountain never seemed to be crowded, not being central and only leading to the Northern wastes. Mary was still gazing at the table, twisting her fingers together and screwing up her face like her daughter, careless of expressing her feelings; what was going on? And yet, he knew what she was going to talk about; why should he get involved? After a lifetime of watching friends twist and turn in their relationships, he felt a little weary, happy to enjoy his simpler friendships and not be drawn into advice, judgment or criticism. But it became clear; he was needed at least to be a friendly ear.

'Oh dear, Matthew, I'm lost, I don't know what to do.'

He said nothing, sighed inwardly. Here it comes. She flung her hands out in appeal, pushed away her coffee and stared directly into his face. How melodramatic; there is little difference between mother and daughter. He could imagine Mari making similar gestures, possibly with fewer words. But Mary surprised him; he had assumed that she was more stoical, unfazed by emotional upsets. What could she possibly want of him? Wife to his son, he knew where his affections lay and couldn't have Mary disrupt the family. He didn't know her, not at all.

'Edward has accused Daniel of sleeping with Elizabeth; it's absurd. I mean, look at Daniel, bless him. Liz is so tight and organised, and Daniel ... well, he's all over the place, isn't he? Can't even organise a holiday; who do you think booked the campsite? Can you imagine Daniel with Liz? Oh dear.' A chuckle.

He couldn't but then he could rarely imagine how couples came together; it had been a repeated surprise to him. Beth used to chide him, claim that she had seen the attraction between friends, wasn't it obvious? With an effort, he could remember Beth entrapping him when they were students. It had seemed easy going along with her, following the trail into marriage, work, life. What would it have been like if he had struck out, left his middle-class education and training – and Isobel – and come up here to the hills and the North to work as a ...

Mary sniffed.

Matthew shifted in his chair, dragged himself back. Edward had written to him in June about his fears and suspicions and he was sad that Edward had persisted in accusing Daniel with such little evidence; a train ticket. But he was not going to tell this to Mary. Had Edward spoken to Elizabeth about his suspicions? It wasn't as if she had never had affairs; Edward had told him so. Wasn't it all up to them? He smiled, reflecting that he had never got mixed up with other women. What a relief.

'It's not funny. Oh dear! I don't know what to do.' She slapped the table with frustration.

'I'm sorry.'

'It's Edward. I told you; he has accused Daniel of having an affair with Elizabeth.'

'Sounds unlikely, doesn't it? Has Daniel said anything to you?'

'He just denies it, of course. And really, you know, I can't believe it of him; I don't think that he has either the imagination or the effort. Or time, I suppose.'

She hesitated and looked away. How attractive and demonstrative she was, in a warm way in spite of her tense expression. No, he didn't know her at all. There was long pause; the background chatter and clinking interrupted his thoughts and he beckoned to the waitress for more coffee. She knew him well enough not to speak, merely scrutinising Mary as though she was a potential conquest.

'Well,' she said, 'he didn't … I don't know … hasn't … couldn't have …'

'I expect it's all a big mistake. Why don't you leave Edward and Elizabeth to sort it out? Daniel can look after himself; he'll get back with Edward in time. Have some cake.'

'Oh Matthew, it wasn't him. No. But of course, Edward has to play the cuckolded husband, all self-righteous, the ass! It isn't even as if he keeps Liz happy; God knows.' She stopped, a stricken look on her face.

'Oh dear, I oughtn't to have said that, ought I? I'm sorry, I can speak privately to you, can't I?'

He laughed at her sad face. 'You can talk to me. I don't know whether I can be much help. But talk away.'

She pushed away her fresh coffee. 'Did you know … no, I'm sure you can't. But you know, Edward doesn't have a very high libido.'

'I expect he spends all his efforts working. I spoke to him recently; he seemed tied up in work.'

'I don't know what it is exactly, I haven't asked, but Liz hasn't been very happy recently. I meet her at exhibitions, you know, and she has been talking about it. She tells me all sorts of things; we get on well.'

What a surprise; Mary had told him that she didn't mix well with Edward, or Elizabeth. She seemed ill at ease when he saw them together; she wasn't at university with them and Daniel, and was the only one currently not to go out to work. So what had happened to change the dynamic? He couldn't imagine Mary and Elizabeth together; Elizabeth had been so

... so managing, so organised. And much as he loved his daughter-in-law, she had never seemed organised. Perhaps that was unfair; he had spent little time in their home, but the home ... no, not organised. Must put such judgemental thoughts out of my mind.

'It must be good to get away from Reading, now and then.'

'Oh, it is. I love it.'

'Elizabeth must be very busy in Chambers; she told me she is working for QC.'

'It's not Daniel.'

'Eh? Well, that must be good to know. So you can leave the others to sort it out? No need to get involved and all that.'

'Well.' She smiled shyly, absurdly.

He sighed inwardly; oh lord, she has been concealing something. It's not very fair on me. Here it comes.

'Elizabeth doesn't have time for a man.' Mary looked proud.

'Edward's got the wrong end of the stick. I'm sure it will sort out in time.'

'It's not quite like that.'

God, this woman is driving me to ... I'm not guessing, if that is what she wants. How soon can we leave?

'I know what it's all about,' she said.

She smiled, a Cheshire cat, sipped her coffee, and sat back, looking round.

'It's nice here, isn't it?' She said, seeing the café for the first time. A long pause and they drank in silence. She turned to him, leaning forward in her seat with an unexpected intensity. In her eyes was a glint of passion, an unexpected ardour, exposed, vulnerable, daring. He couldn't return her look but dropped his eyes to his cup.

'It was me.'

He looked at her and then out of the window, following the flight of a thrush as it rose over the roofs and disappeared. How pleasant it would be to fly, to rise one thousand feet without effort and lay upon the hills, free of ... But then there was his painting and his curiosity and his need of people. What does one say?

He coughed. 'You?'

'It was me.' She smiled and he saw relief passing over her like a cloud shadow, her body relaxing, slumping in the seat. She took a piece of Matthew's cake and crumbled it on her plate; he felt like withdrawing, taking off to the hills. Now. This moment. It wasn't fair; it was no business of his.

An explosive giggle burst out of her. 'Oh Matthew, I've shocked you, haven't I? Oh dear, I don't believe that you are really an old fuddy-duddy, are you?'

Old fuddy-duddy indeed! 'But. You said she is so tight and organized. And she's a barrister. And –'

The glow of pride that shone from her lit the table, scalding him. 'Oh, and I love it, the tightness and organisedness! Do you know what it's like at home?

Children's games, clothes, lessons, mess, … you've seen it, and Daniel! Sometimes I feel as though he has forgotten me. Oh, I love him but I feel that I'm on a shelf, waiting for him to have time for me. He comes and goes, sometimes bringing crowds of academics, papers all over the place, sometimes local politicians fawning on him for advice; I'm sick of it, all the mess. The children are fine, they don't notice, but I get the brunt of it.'

She sat back exhausted, eyes down, a tear washing away her smile.

'I'm so tired of it all, the mother bit and the housekeeper bit and nothing else. It is such a treat, so unexpected. And now the stress; I don't know what to do.'

He took her hand and gazed out of the window. A blackbird landed on the window cill, cocked its head, and stared at them with a glassy eye. She sniffed, grasping his hand with both of hers. A tear dropped onto his hand and he watched it dribble to the table. He felt exhausted himself, unwilling to advise or exercise care.

'Oh dear, I can't keep it secret any longer; will you tell Daniel for me? I just can't, I don't know where to start and I'm afraid.'

He should be tough, tell her to pull herself together. He could ignore her, tell her to get on with her life. He could … He didn't know what to say. Try a mundane question.

'How do you find the time, with the family and cooking?'

'Oh, I go up to London for the day occasionally, to see exhibitions. Only we don't always go to exhibitions; sometimes, well quite a lot recently, we go to a small hotel Liz knows near Marble Arch and drink and eat and go to bed together. It's wonderful; I didn't know it was possible. It's a release, I didn't know what it would be like, it makes me feel human, no, more than that. And Liz is so good, so …'

She paused, drank coffee, smiled, picking at a spot on the table.

'We were at an exhibition of Fauve art; do you know it? There was a Schille, all legs and limbs and cocks and bare bodies and Liz stopped and stared at it for ages. I thought she was going to say something about the man but she said how sexy the woman was and how she wished she could be there. I thought that they were both rather bony, I was really surprised, I didn't expect her to say that. We went for coffee later and she talked about how frustrated she was and how affairs with men were so impossible – they were all possessive and threatening – and how she wanted a nice comforting physical relationship and still have Edward for partner sex. He has a low sperm count, you know, that's why they don't have children. I don't know what I said. She took my hand and we gazed at each other for ages. And then we kissed, right there in the café. And that's how it started; she organized everything, it's wonderful. She even sends me train tickets. And you are the first person I have been able to tell.'

He didn't know whether to feel grateful for this confidence, to distant himself or to ask questions. It was as though a storm had burst over the town, a thunder of relationships, men with men, women with women, parents and children, old friends and him. He couldn't speak, seeking to escape back to an ordinary Keswick day with a dull sky and wondered what he would cook for supper.

After a while, she said quietly, 'Matthew, please, can you help me? Oh dear, I don't know what to do. Can you tell Daniel?'

He gazed at her; she was a different person. Now she took up significant space, created a bow wave before her to be navigated around. No longer could she be the subdued housewife and mother. More alive to him, she shimmered with unknown depths and colours. And still he wanted to be elsewhere, not involved, not trapped. And it was his family, his son, his daughter-in-law, and, not to be forgotten, his grandchildren.

'Mary, what do you want? Do you know what you want? There are so many aspects to this –'

'Oh, that's simple,' she burst out, 'I want my new life, I want the pleasure and the escape from … from … all that at home and … and I want my family and my husband too and … and they want me.'

'And how do you think Daniel will react to the news? What will he say to Edward?'

There was a minefield to be negotiated. Might everyone come out of the dénouement without pain? He doubted it, sensing possession and demands and jealousy. That is how he would have felt if Isobel had told him she was having an affair with ... a man ... or a woman ... it was very difficult to imagine.

Mary was rattling on. 'I don't know; it's not as if I was having an affair with a colleague of his or somebody else. It's not as if there haven't been opportunities. I could have had an affair on campus I suppose; they happen all the time, you know, but it's so dreary, the same old round of lecturers and staff. I know, it's odd, isn't it? Why a woman? Well, women know what is satisfying and being gentle with each other. Oh, I know, they can also be complete bitches, catty, sniping, petty and destructive. Perhaps they have a wider sensual range than men. And I can't speak for all women, only Liz and myself. It just works, that's all. And we don't need to involve anybody else; we still have our partners, homes and family.'

'Astonishing! I have never heard it explained before but then I have never really thought about lesbian affairs. I suppose your relationship doesn't involve love?' He had read and thought of such things, but felt a natural withdrawal from the politics of it, the questions and problems.

Mary bridled at his words. 'We are very fond of each other and we both need something. It's convenient, supportive, satisfying and refreshing and it doesn't get in the way of our lives. At least not until Edward started behaving so stupidly!' She paused. 'And I don't think of us as lesbians. It's not the kind of full-time love for a partner; we have that already.'

'But that is more important isn't it, the marriage?' Surely, she could see that.

'Of course, and the family.'

He felt a hardness growing, a reluctance to give in to the wish to have it all.

'You know, I wouldn't be so sure that the children don't have suspicions; I thought Mari looked a little strained and she was watching you like a hawk at lunch.'

'Oh, she's just a temperamental teenager, that's all.'

'Have you forgotten what it is like to be a child, living in the shadow of your parents? Seeing, watching and learning from them? I wouldn't be so sure.'

Mary dropped her head and was silent.

'Why can't you ask Elizabeth to call Edward off Daniel? To tell him all. Don't you think that she has had affairs before? Edward must have some idea.'

'She has, she told me. She said she told Edward that she was spending time with another woman but he refused to believe it. It's bizarre, he would have believed it if it had been a man but when she told him it was a woman, he thought that it was bluff to put him off the scent. He knows she's not a lesbian and he can't imagine another kind of relationship.'

He thought of Edward and he thought of Daniel

and tried not to think of Elizabeth and Mary. He loved Daniel, was sorry to think of him hurt. He would have liked to take him up on a mountain and talk to him about hills and clouds and sheep and women and sex. But it was not his place.

'You see,' he explained gently, 'I can't tell Daniel; it's not my place. You will have to do it yourself.'

'But how? How can I avoid hurting him? What is he going to think?'

'Hurt him? Won't it be worse if … You'll have to do it yourself you know. Just get it out, weather the storm. It's never as bad as one fears.' There were no other comfortable sayings that he could summon. It sounded unconvincing. Tough, that was how life could be. You took risks; you took life above the quiet monotone of mundanity and you could fall off a cliff. In business, on the hills, in personal relationships.

Shortly afterwards, they left the café. Mary appeared to have lost her appetite for shopping and stood by listlessly while he picked up some food for an early supper. They returned to a quiet house; Daniel was reading to the boys, Mari sitting to one side with a book open. Matthew asked her to help him prepare supper and she sprang up at once, purposeful and full of help. What had she been listening to? He was surprised at the answer: Monteverdi, The Rolling Stones, Sonny Rollins. Did she know what she wanted to be, and was told that it was far too early to decide that, she might know when she had finished at Oxford, her father's old College, naturally. She smiled briefly, a glint of her mother. It was likely, he thought, that she would know before then.

When he thought that they were leaving, Mary sent the children to play. Matthew was washing up, happy alone in his kitchen. As he walked in to clear some dishes, he heard Mary said, 'Daniel, I have something to tell you. You know Edward accused you of having an affair with Liz?'

'Absurd! When would I have time to go to London for an affair? Not that Liz is unattractive, but not my sort ...'

'Oh, I know, darling.' Mary paused, looked at Matthew, gave a little smile, and carried on. 'Of course it's not you. It's me.'

Matthew felt uncomfortable immediately, drawn into a private matter; damn Mary, it was unfair. He watched his son Daniel, who stared, silent, his face a raw untreated canvas, no expression, eyes blind.

'Edward found a train ticket to Reading and decided that it was you,' said Mary. 'But it was me, all the time. Edward won't accept that his wife has had, is having a relationship with a woman.' It was astonishing; Mary's voice was level, a slight wobble the only sign of doubt, of fear. She sounded more as if she were comforting Daniel, reassuring him, rather than leading him into a mire. But was it a mire? Matthew found it all too confusing and withdrew to the kitchen. Unfortunately, the kitchen was directly adjacent to the diningroom; he couldn't help overhearing every word, even though he was no longer present in their conversation. He stood still, unwilling to draw notice by washing; he could hear his heart pumping and leaned upon the surface. Poor Daniel; how could Mary convince him that there was no harm to their marriage?

He heard Daniel loud, not understanding. 'What are you talking about? We've been married for nearly twenty years. You've never shown any interest in women … I don't understand.'

And Mary falter.

'Oh dear, I don't know where to start. It's so complicated … I want you to know I love you, and the children.'

'But what's wrong? Have I done something or failed to do something?' Daniel sounded questioning, rather than angry. This must be an unknown sea for him to set out on, unknown perils. Matthew wished he could silence Mary, and yet at the same time wanted it all to be out in the open.

'Yes, and no. I just want more to life than being the mother at home, washing dirty socks and cooking endless meals, and being there for you all while you come and go. Can you understand that, do you know what I mean?'

'But that's what you have always wanted, not to work and be there for the children. What do you mean 'more to life'?'

Daniel sounded very confused; Matthew could

imagine him running his hands through his hair, frowning at the table. And he could do nothing for him.

'Daniel, my darling, you and the children are everything to me –'

'Obviously not!' Daniel sounded hurt, rather than angry.

'Let me finish, please. I don't love you any the less but there is something inside me that wants more for life, for myself. So I went to exhibitions with Liz and that was great, and then … ' Mary faded into silence.

'Don't you think you should give me some sort of explanation, some sort of sense to it all? Where's the logic?'

A pause. Silence. He heard Mary sniff and wondered if she was going to break down in tears again. Oh come on Daniel. What is logic to do with it? There's a professor but where's reality?

'My love, when did you last spend a whole evening with me alone, a relaxing intimate evening?'

Daniel was silent. Was he thinking of his failings as a loving husband, or wondering where his wife had gone, into ways of which he had no knowledge or understanding?

Mary continued, 'I don't wish to lose any part of you, our children or our home but I feel the need to grow, to have more to life than cooking and washing; more also than our occasional lovemaking. I want to be appreciated for who I am; I want to feel more physically, more sensually. I don't know, perhaps I want too much; perhaps I am being unfair to you. But you see, I don't feel any less love for you but I feel more alive now, more satisfied.'

Daniel sounded angry now, as though on firm ground. 'Is this sex as important as that? How did it start?'

'Please, I don't understand it all myself. It's not just sex. It is so different, you see, and I feel comfortable and released with it.'

Mary described briefly how it had started and repeated how she loved him just the same as always.

'So do you see it carrying on as it is now for ... for ... sometime?' Daniel sounded confused.

'I don't know, Daniel. I don't know anything. I don't know myself. It's all so new. That's how things are.' Mary sounded exhausted. He heard her slump into a chair.

'I should like to feel that I am enough for my wife, that I satisfy her. Do I really not spend much time with you? ... No, I suppose not. But you know what working life and family life is like. I feel exhausted quite a lot of the time but I wouldn't want to spend less time with the children.'

'What do you want, Daniel?'

'I don't know; this is all a little sudden. Can we talk about it?'

'We are, my love, we are, thank goodness.'

There was a pause; Matthew could imagine Daniel trying to adjust and wondered whether he was still angry. He willed him to be open, to tell Mary what he wanted.

'Well,' he said. 'I want you and the children, and my work and our friends. And I want holidays and to travel and a larger house would be nice, and –'

'But it doesn't work like that, does it? The days are not long enough; there is only so much of yourself that you can give. How much do you want to give to your family and how much to your work?' Mary sounded strained. Matthew wondered why she hadn't added 'how much to your wife'.

'Oh Mary, have I been so selfish or inattentive?'

'No, and yes. I know you don't mean to but you get taken away, distracted by all those people who make demands on you and we don't make those demands. We love you and support you but we would like more of you, all of us but especially me.' Mary's voice broke

There was a long pause and Matthew heard movement, probably Daniel.

'I'm so sorry, don't weep,' said Daniel. 'What should I do? I must teach, that's our income, so what should I do?'

'Could you spend less time with the local Party? And less time with your discussion groups? You wanted to publish; could you do more at home and spend more time with us? I think Mari in particular would appreciate some time with you.'

Matthew smiled to himself; so Mary had taken that on board.

'Mari? Really? I had no idea, I thought she wanted to be an independent outrageous teenager and have nothing to do with her father.'

'Oh Daniel, my love, she needs you even more now; she's just getting to know the world and you are both her father and a man and she wants to learn.'

'And you? Can things be different with you?'

'What do you think? Where are you Daniel or where have you been? Do you not remember how we were when we were young? Do you remember ... No, we've been following our own paths, haven't we? But things could change. Shall we see? Gosh, it's late, we must go, where are the children? Poor Matthew, I think we banished him from his own room.'

At some stage, Matthew was not quite sure when, he saw Mari in the kitchen with him; at first, he thought that she had come to ask some music question but then he noticed that she was fiddling with things on the side. Had she heard her parents' discussion? It would not have been a good idea; she would probably have got the wrong end of the stick. Really Mary! She should take more care. He took Mari gently by the arm and walked her back to his study, asking whether there was anything that she would like.

'Oh, it's all right. I just came to ask you a question about jazz but it can wait for now.'

She seemed distracted; possibly, she had heard too much of her parents' conversation but there was nothing that he could do about that, nothing that he could say unless she appealed for help. He returned to the kitchen.

Mary came looking for him; her eyes shone with a new light but she did not speak. Probably she suspected that he had been obliged to listen to all their conversation. She gripped his hands and he smiled and gave her a kiss.

'It was lovely to see you all and to meet the children. I like them; you can leave them here if you and Daniel would like some time to yourselves.'

'Thankyou, Matthew, I hope you meant it, I would like to take you up on that soon.'

'How about the day after tomorrow? I can give them lunch and a walk or something. Do you think Mari will be happy?'

'She'll be fine, don't worry about that. It'll do her good, a bit of different company.'

They left in a rush, back to their tent. As the dust settled, and the cat reappeared, he recalled that he had heard nothing of the visit to the Pencil Museum. Well, perhaps the boys would fill him in when they came for lunch.

CHAPTER 7

Early August

Home at last, back from Chambers. Exhausted. Off the streets, it was quiet and cool. No Edward, thank goodness. No house-keepers, no cleaners, nobody; must be their time off. A grateful still silence with a faint smell of fresh blossoms and the constant suppressed murmur of Islington like a distant orchestra tuning up. She sank into a chair, kicked her shoes off; her mind drifted, cleared itself from work. Muscles rearranged themselves, heartbeat ticked over, that irritable tic vanishing, a coolness massaged her face. Droop.

I could sleep ...Shoes ... oh, Mariana can find them, ought to give her a day off ...bed, I want bed to lie flat, softness, dark above my head, swinging around at anchor, giving in and then oh the sun in Spain caresses, not dusty like London, and leads into a soft naked place Mediterranean seen between my feet in those funny espadrilles under the parasol, wonderful bright glazed tiles and all that contorted ironwork, brilliant colours and the smell, so hot all the time, until ... until it's time to cast it all off to swim and sleep, sleep and swim, funny clothes shops, better naked, feel that air move from the sea over my back breasts tickle down there roll over cool tiles towel hot, on the balcony alone possibly it doesn't matter no effort body to sleep and ... to stroll out just like that if I could invisible who cares ... sharp smell of oranges, orange evening sun over a dark endless sea, felt free, dark continent to the South strange smells skin scented sounds drifting a drum-beat... later floating on the limits of alcohol, head above my body free, turn to see strange colours and dark doorways children hiding, always twisting steps upwards to places I can't see, places where it all goes on, touching, a lick, can't see, smells that I don't know, taste, I want to see, but float away, smells of food, that tapas stuff but not now, not here ... oh ... oh bugger, must move

Edward drank too much brewer's droop isn't in it poor bugger, that reminded her, must book this summer, at least they agreed on that place, knew what it's like, where to go ...

Edward, I don't know, where is he now with us, us, what do I mean, husband and wife, talks of freezing his balls off in the Lakes, Matthew's OK but for God's sake ... but if it was just me, oh, if it was just me ... away to Paris, not August, but Paris in the springtime autumn winter, stay some small private hotel, few friends, close, intimate and go out, talk and touch, a little intimate exploration, what was that shop where they have those ... God, I want a rest, Chambers so busy, can't the Clerk send some cases another way, yes I know he's trying to help me with the QC application, does the Chambers good, reputation and all that another QC and then they work us but ...I haven't told them, have I, won't but will take my time off, get over the Channel when I can ought to buy a little place, where maybe the 7th arrondissement I don't know, someone will tell me ... and that case today, funny the Judge looking at me like that, don't know what I did but that poor bastard in the dock, when will men learn about women and not take them for granted ... want to be taken for granted now and then, need it, want it, bed, oh Mary, Mary where are you now when I ... If only she wasn't so boring that little house in Reading, boys and clothes and Daniel and cooking ... who was that solicitor in Chambers, told he came in for a con, what firm, looked rather dishy and not too nice, wonder if he's married, make a note of it to ask Jean ... and our Clerk, dear boy, always trying to load me with extra cases so my QC application will look good but not that driving prosecution, God no, better remember to look at the papers, find something for my pupil ... Oh no, is that the front door bell? Forget it. Let them ring. Bugger off. Can't be important, not Chambers I hope. Oh God, is it those papers for tomorrow? And I said ... bugger

Staggered up. What, what, oh no, couldn't leave the bell alone whoever it is ... couldn't see anything, these bloody peepholes are useless ...

Edward said they had to have one, why isn't the entry phone working, all that money, people don't use them, bloody thing ... not one of those bloody children from the estates looking for trouble, I'll get the ... looks like someone is sitting on the doorstep ... like those women in the Tube, babies and all ... looks a bit like Mari but couldn't be her, dear goddaughter ... just becoming interesting, possibilities, a woman one day soon, can't stand children hanging round your ankles and the mess, Mary's house just impossible, why doesn't she do something about it, a bomb might help ... why does Mari always wear those awful clothes, bloody teenager, must take her to Paris and dress her properly, could change her life, wouldn't look back, awful trouble I'd be in what a laugh but she needs it, look at her ... got an idea what would go well with her pale colouring and all that hair, beautiful hair, but so much of it, take her out of herself, introduce her to things the world art food clothes ... bet she doesn't have a boyfriend too busy reading dear girl, just becoming interesting ... that Bayswater Hotel is great isn't it, just quiet enough for two, wonder if they wonder, probably know why we are there, that wall-paper and the smell of their soap and the smell of ... images of her stretched naked on a bed, moving, smiling, bombard me, tease me ... oh Mary, you're too demanding you're just getting tiresome, time you were gone … but not yet …. perhaps Mary would like some of those clothes of mine, they'd suit her … take her to Paris, Rive Gauche that funny little boutique, so discreet, fun, funny, go there … next year? Who is on the doorstep?

There was a knock on the door. Persistent. Difficult time, odd hour for a caller; ignore it; concentrate on getting away from the day's court case, away from the tangle between husband and wife that is unravelling by degrees. Who would call at this hour except some wretched cold caller, seeking to sell something bloody useless? Got everything I want, haven't I? Except for … Oh hell, there was the bell again.

She peered through the spyhole again.

At first she couldn't see anyone; then become aware again of a tangle of hair below. Yes, someone was sitting on the step, an orphan perhaps or a waif and stray begging for a meal. With a groan, she opened the door an inch on the chain and peered out. The cool vanished; it was a noisy, horrible, sunny afternoon and she retreated a little as the person below rose and turned towards her.

'Mari!'

She was astounded; never seen her away from her parents before, never in London. Was she casting herself on her godmother in a fit of pique at some familial rejection? Her parents, well … Or was she lost on some school trip? Must be holidays. She opened the door and drew the girl to her, hugging her out of the street. Cool again. Mari pulled back, didn't say anything, looking at the floor. Horrible clothes; is this what she wears? What was that smell? Sort of burnt. Flies in her hair or is it leaves? Without a word, she led her to the kitchen and switched on the kettle. Mari started to talk but Elizabeth stopped her. Had to get used to her being here by herself; couldn't remember the last time she was here. She was bigger, more like a person, than a part of her parents. Small breasts, but cute waist; she would dress well. Put her at her ease.

'Wait a minute, have a drink and something to eat. Then we'll sit down.'

Mari raised her hands as though surrendering, took a biscuit and ate it slowly, catching the crumbs in her hand. She shrugged her jacket onto the floor, her bag onto a chair. It was large, more like a sack, heavy with books and God knows what else.

Mind you, Elizabeth thought, when I was at school, when I was the perfect single child, my parents never knew what was in my bag, what I carried around: condoms – a boy gave them to me – sweets, a map of London for when I was going to escape – I never did – sanitary stuff and books, magazines, letters. I wonder if Mari gets letters or cards from some admirer; she's a damn sight more attractive than I was.

She picked up the jacket and hung it over the back of a chair. Mari stood as though stunned, looking round the immaculate kitchen, at the cooker that was so clean that it looked as if it had never been used, the sparkling chrome equipment displayed on the granite surfaces, the large table by the garden doors with the six armchairs and the modern oil paintings. She sighed. Elizabeth sensed it was out of frustration, or perhaps envy, a different world from her home. Poor dear.

It is, thought Elizabeth, a perfect paradise for a couple that works their socks off simply to get away from it as often as possible. Strange, I can almost imagine it as pictures in an upmarket estate agent, crisp and perfect, not a spot of dirt or wear. We always end up doing business entertaining elsewhere and rarely have guests.

She picked up a tray with mugs and biscuits and led the way upstairs to her dressing room. Mari tried to pick up her bag.

'It will all right there. There's no-one here.'

Upstairs, she pushed Mari into the comfortable armchair, pulled up a stool, looked into her face. She had grown since their last meeting; the teenage clothes and the childish unruly hair sat like a veil over a more mature person who was beginning to emerge. A firmness and determination that was new; Elizabeth remembered Mari as a child, easy to please, grateful for any gift or attention, polite, sometimes distant, occasionally lost to books or music. She wondered whether she really knew her. The sudden childlike gestures were gone. There was little sign of the teenage rebelliousness, the evasion and rudeness. She moved differently; she could be graceful, if she knew how. Well.

'It's lovely to see you. It's been ages. Does Mary know you are here?'

'I came straight from a friend's; I didn't want to get stuck.'

'Stuck? Is anything wrong? Have you had anything to eat?'

'I'm OK. Really. I needed to talk to you.'

'What is it? Have you had some trouble with a boy, or at home?'

She racked her memory for the problems that plagued her youth, wondered how much things had changed. She didn't remember much but then she had lived a very sheltered life, private schools and all. Not that home was exactly lively. A different country from Mary's house. She had no idea what her own mother did all day. Apart from play bridge. And smoke. And drink cocktails. What sort of life went with those things? She didn't want to imagine it. She hadn't liked her, hadn't known her. So having no brothers or sisters or children of her own, she had to work hard to imagine how the world might affect her goddaughter; she assumed that the transition through teenage years was as hard as ever, that nobody understood, parents in particular. But her school, and boys, and all that; not a world she knew at all.

She could stay the night and talk and Elizabeth would help her. That was what godmothers were for.

Edward would see her to a morning train. The court case would prevent her from doing that small duty of care. It was nice to think of her coming here, coming to her godmother; she warmed to her, wanted to help. They could do things together, soon, in a year or so. With exasperation she thought of Mary's household, of the continual mess and coming and going, the oddly dressed teenagers from Mari's school mixing with Daniel's scruffy students and suited local politicians; how could Mary run any sort of ordered household in that situation? Bless her, she had been an amenable bed companion, sometimes even surprising. But a little too demanding and not ultimately satisfying. It had been an interesting experiment, a novel experience and quite fun at times. But time to move on. One day.

Mari looked better, more composed.

'No, it's alright, I'm all right. But I need your help. It's a bit difficult. But you said that I could always talk to you about things that I might not want to with Mum and Dad.'

'Shouldn't we ring home, tell them that you are here? They'll be worried, won't they?'

'Must we? What's the time? Could we talk first?'

'I don't know what time they expect you but Mary will be worried, won't she?'

Mari ignored her; she seemed so sure that she would have her attention. She felt a prickle of concern; was she pregnant? She's old enough. They always said that the quiet ones got into trouble first, not the noisy sociable confident ones that used to be in the bar at College, making most noise, chatting up men. Or is it something to do with the University? Is it some colleague of Daniel's who has been making inappropriate approaches?

'I think Mum's having an affair, she disappears some days and we don't see her until supper. And Dad's gone all vague and doesn't seem to hear her talking. I don't know what to do.'

Elizabeth was still. The background buzz of traffic sounded loud, bruising, through the faint resonance of the house around her. Between them, she felt an invisible barrier, balking messages that were not interpretable. Not wanted. She looked at Mari; did she know? Her face gave nothing away; she looked like an innocent young teenager, earnest, a little hidden. It was the hidden bit that was always misleading. Where did it come from? Upbringing or change of life? After all she was 14 now, a rapid change would be picking her up from childhood, swinging her around, shaking up all her beliefs, in life, parents, friendships ... godmother ...

Elizabeth was still. She wanted to get away from her. Bugger Mary, what had she done? I knew it went on too long, encouraged her so she got sloppy, careless. Dangerous. I don't like my affairs public, thank you very much. I like my privacy, my own private world. With whoever I please. And I don't really want to be upsetting Daniel's family.

Mari was gazing at the floor. For a moment Elizabeth wanted to slap her, eradicate her words, take them back to where they were. She didn't want a knowing Mari, a calculating Mari; she wanted a beautiful young compliant friend who she could take in hand, introduce to a soft sensual life, who would be a companion to her as she grew older. Bugger it.

Mari must be mistaken; she can't have heard about it.

'Are you sure you're right? She's probably studying or something, doing an art history course.'

Mari looked at her. Elizabeth knew that she had never before had to discuss anything of importance with her and hold her own view. With her legal skills, Elizabeth thought she could quite easily turn her; divert her from her purpose. Probably. She even wondered whether Mari thought that her mother's affair had not actually been a bad thing, whether she believed that her mother was enjoying the escape from home life, that life had become intolerable without it.

But, like many children, she probably believed that her mother's life belonged to the family and Mari's main concerns would be for her father who needed help, was incapable of looking after his own life; and for herself. She would not want her own life disrupted; she would nurture her need for a stable time during her last years at home so that she could get into Oxford. Quite calculating, really. And flourish, grow way beyond her home background, follow in the footsteps of her father and possibly go further. Her parents would have to be brought together and made to bond, to run a family home. She was bright, Elizabeth had always known that, and she began to feel concern for her.

How often at work have I wanted to drag the offending couples together, bang their heads together and tell them to stop their expensive destructive tearing-apart? She didn't for a moment consider her role in this family drama; it was as though it was happening to clients, not directly involved with her own private life. It was Mary's fault and Elizabeth felt absolved of all responsibility. Anyway, now we must play a little drama, dance a little jig over the death of my affair and then go out and celebrate. Some celebration.

'Surely, you are mistaken. Do you have any idea who it might be? How can she have time?'

'I'm sure of it; she has new knickers like never before and she seems sort of happy and distracted. She never hears us when we talk to her and there seems to be no communication with Dad at all. I think he has been sleeping in his study. Or somewhere else. But I don't know who it is, no idea.'

Mari appeared to have an odd look and the idea grew that she knew all about the affair. She didn't know her well enough but she suspected that Mari had learnt to become an efficient liar; goodness knows how but after all she, Elizabeth, had been a pretty good liar from the age of 12. Part of growing up with her parents. She groaned inwardly; oh Mary, did you have to flaunt my generosity, just a little sexy present? She must be talking about me; can't believe that Mary has another lover; I just can't believe that of her. How could Mary be so stupid, why couldn't she keep it to herself? Oh well, it was going to end soon. This seems a good excuse, remind Mary of her family responsibilities, say how sorry I am, move on. Start all over again, somebody somewhere. But I can't tell Mari that. 'How serious do you think it is?'

Mari looked quite proud; what was going on? Did she see herself as the guardian angel, looking after the family, rounding them up and corralling them? Supposing that she knew who it was and didn't want to accuse me, alienate her loving and very generous godmother ...

'Oh, I think Daddy thinks it's very serious and Mummy just doesn't seem to care! But it's really important; they love each other; and us.'

The laying down of facts, unassailable; she might make a barrister in time. Did she know how frustrated her mother had been? Did she have the slightest inkling of how Mary had been like a smouldering bonfire, bursting into full flame with a little encouragement? God, it had been quite exhausting at time. She wished that she could tell Mari, let her know that her mother was a woman with a woman's needs. The needs that she would feel before long. But it won't do; it'll have to wait a few years. She's a junior, under 16, and it doesn't help Daniel's family to split it apart, drag into the light what should never have been buried for so long. Wake up Daniel. Not my job, have to leave it to them. She's being the virtuous daughter looking after her father. I'm tempted to pour scorn on Mari's outburst, tell her that parents often have phases of this sort; she'll see one day. But, somehow, I can't do that to Mari; she has confided in me.

'Shall I talk to your mother? Or your father?'

'No, don't talk to Daddy, it would only upset him. And I don't think it would change anything.'

'Alright, I'll talk to Mary but you realize that I may be intruding into her private life? I can only say that I was concerned about you.'

Mari gave me another odd look and said nothing. Yes, I believe she knows what is going on; how about a bit of bribery?

'When will you be sixteen, Mari? It's time you branched out from home and school, had a bit of life education. I think it would do both of us good to have a little Paris trip, don't you? Buy some clothes, see some art, have a few really good meals. What do you think?'

Marie opened her mouth with amazement.

'Oh, Elizabeth, that would be marvellous! Could we go after GCSEs? I'm sure they would let me go with you.'

She jumped up and hugged me, a fleeting look on her face. Did she think that she was being blackmailed? Silly girl; if only she was ten years older, she probably wouldn't worry about all of this.

'Elizabeth, could you 'phone Mummy and let her know that I'm alright?'

'Of course! I'll call her now and you can go back on the morning train. How about supper out? I'm pooped and I don't feel like cooking; let's go out. Edward can meet us there.'

She left her sitting there, an awkward oddly-dressed teenager in her beautiful dressing room with the door firmly shut, and went downstairs to the kitchen to telephone. One of the boys replied, young and keen. She heard him go through their house, soprano voice trilling 'Mum, Mum! It's Elizabeth!' and after a while Mary was there, a little breathless, uncertain.

'Elizabeth? Is that you?'

'Mary, hullo. How are you?'

'I'm fine, fine. But you never phone; what's the matter?'

'Can you talk? Are you alone?'

'Hang on … just a tick.' She heard boys being dismissed, sent upstairs.

'That's better. What is it?'

'Mari is here. She wanted you to know.'

'Mari? Why? What's she doing? Is she all right? I hadn't missed her, I thought that she was round at Rebecca's.'

'No, she's here and she's fine; or at least, she seems fine. She wanted to talk to me.'

'Mari? What on earth for?'

Elizabeth hesitated; was this the way to do it?

Would a letter be better, less fall-out? She shrugged. Let's get it over with; not fair to Mary to pretend she didn't know when they were talking.

'She told me that her mother is having an affair.'

A long pause. She could hear Mary breathing, coarsely; it reminded her of times together.

'Are you there, Mary? Mary?'

'Wha …at? What did you say?'

Heavy breathing; was she crying?

'She told me that her mother is having an affair. Or she believes she is; often out till supper, new underwear, distracted father. Do I need to go on? Why the bit about the father?'

'How could she? I don't understand, I haven't told anyone, except for Daniel.'

'You had to tell him? I thought you weren't going to.'

'It sort of happened when we were away. I felt all bottled up, I had to say something. I didn't want to upset anyone … well, I didn't know. I didn't like having secrets from Daniel. Oh, Beth.'

'It seems to have got out of hand. Mari doesn't know who the other party is. At least, she said she didn't know.'

'Do you think that she knows? Can you tell?'

'Some funny looks. I must say, if she knows, she is being quite calculating, managing the whole affair … sorry, I shouldn't have used that word.'

'I suppose she overheard me talking to Daniel;

can't think of another time. But where does it leave us?'

'Leave us? How's Daniel?'

'Oh, he's being silly; can't get to him at present. And he keeps working all the time. But we are doing something about that. I think.' She sounded vague; Elizabeth could imagine that Mary had done little to improve things at home.

'What? You tell him you're having an affair and he takes to sleeping in his study, or at least that is what Mari says, but you are doing something about it.' Really Mary, you need to grasp the nettle.

'Oh Beth, don't be angry. I couldn't bear it.'

'It's the end, isn't it?'

'No! No, I can't ... what would I do without you ... no, please ...'

'It's pretty clear, Mary.'

'But we could still meet. I go to London, look at pictures, that sort of thing.'

'Mary, it's pretty clear.'

'And nobody need know.'

'What about Daniel?'

'I'll tell him, it's all over.'

'Until the next time you feel bottled up. It doesn't work, Mary, face it.'

'No, please, let's make it work.'

'It's getting difficult with Daniel, isn't it? He's finding it difficult to adapt. Is he making you choose yet?'

'Not yet but we seem to be getting to that. And I

know what I have to do then. But we haven't got there yet; he is still spending too much time working and I told him, if he wants me, he's got to be there for me. And … Oh! It's all so awful. I don't know what to do!'

Mary was weeping now, loud and unrestrained gulps.

'Hold on, Mary, one thing at a time. What shall I tell Mari?'

There was a long pause at the other end; some sniffing, a cough.

'Please … please, just tell her that I'm glad I know where she is and I love her. How's she getting home?'

'Oh, don't worry about that. She can stay tonight; we'll have a girly time and then Edward will put her on a train tomorrow.'

'I don't know what to do. Dear Beth, I don't want to lose you.'

'But you have to you know. We can't go on like this with Daniel and Mari knowing.' She was gentle; she surprised herself.

'Oh Beth, I've had such good times with you. I never dreamt … couldn't have known what was possible. It was so good!'

'Yes, it was good but it's over. I'll talk to Mari but I shan't tell her about it. You must make her feel more secure, you and Daniel.'

'Of course, Beth. Thanks for 'phoning. I'll talk to you soon.'

'Bye, Mary. Look after yourself; and Daniel.'

That was over. Not a new situation; she had plenty of experience in that sort of thing. But Mary; afraid she might have hurt her. She was one of those needy people who have difficulty finding the right person. As for herself, Elizabeth thought, Edward would never change. She would have to look elsewhere for a mutually interested person. Preferably male. Easier to get rid of if they became difficult; or boring.

Mari was asleep, curled up in the chair; she looked young and vulnerable and Elizabeth sighed at the destruction caused unwittingly by the young upon their elders. When she had changed, she woke her, sent her off for a shower and had fun dressing her up for the evening; Mari loved it, revelled in clothes that she would never own, even picked out a little jewellery. It was astonishing, the transformation. The teenage cloak was stripped away; Elizabeth stood her in her underwear and offered her one garment at a time, making her look in the mirror to see what effect it had upon her. And she brushed her red hair, again and again; what a luscious colour, what a lucky girl. Elizabeth would have liked to have seen it cut. At first, Mari was shy, unappreciative of those strange skirts that changed her so much. She began to turn and walk a little, feeling the change and wanting to try others. Once she laughed at an apparition that she could not recognise. Eventually, they settled on a compromise, what fitted and what Mari wanted.

Edward never appeared at the restaurant. Mari

didn't eat very much; Elizabeth assumed that she was weary, exhausted after their conversation. But the meal brought strength and she revived. They chatted about holidays, clothes, hair, and boys.

'What will you read at Oxford, Mari? Not too early to be thinking about it, you know.'

She blinked; she was caught unawares. Yet she couldn't believe that Daniel has not brought up university courses; how old is she now? 14?

'Which way do you lean? Towards arts or sciences? You have to do both at the moment, don't you?'

'Yes, GCSEs in masses of subjects but they're not too difficult. I have a friend who doesn't really bother; her problem is that she is too clever and she says that as long as she passes, why bother to do masses of work. But I'm not so sure; isn't it a good idea to get used to working, for A levels and University?'

'Of course. But remember that the universities like a well-rounded student, one who knows a little of the world and is not afraid to express her own opinions, well, to have opinions, on politics, literature, music and so on. Do you read a newspaper?'

'No. But I see the news on the television. What should I read?'

'Any good spreadsheet; Daniel reads the Guardian? Try that. It's quite easy, particularly for you. And what about travel? Always broadens the mind. Paris next summer?'

'I'll only be 15, you know. First year of GCSEs.'

'I think it's quite old enough to come to Paris with me. Bring you out a bit. Mary won't worry; she'll be jealous, I should think. And we can look at a little art, talk about books and go to some boutiques. No, you are not to worry about money; I have enough, good gracious, and I would like to help you. Happy with that?'

At which Mari fell about, embarrassed and awkward, still young but going to be interesting if she had anything to do with it. She just needed a little direction from outside the home; Elizabeth doubted whether Daniel had enough time to realise that his daughter was growing up and that he should be considering her future. Putting a word in here and there; she would. Don't think Mary knows that world so well; not likely to push her in the right direction. Suddenly, Mari spoke up.

'Can you tell me who I should read? School books are a bit simple and I get bored. Are there any authors that you recommend?'

She was taken aback. After telling her to read, she had to confess that she didn't have much time for reading and had fallen out of the habit, except on holiday when she read easy literature. So she promised to look out some books and send them to her; she knew somebody who would help. Mari didn't need to know that they would all be new books, straight from the shop.

'Do you write letters?'

'Oh yeah, we all do. Cards mostly. But I don't do much; they spend an awful lot of time on them.'

'Well, suppose that you write to me and we'll communicate a little. About the world and things. Would you do that?'

Again, she was so pleased that Elizabeth began to feel guilty at what her expectations might be and whether she could satisfy them. Well, time will tell. Eventually they got to bed, Mari in a nightie of hers, and the next morning she left her in Edward's hands. He had strict instructions to take her to the station but to stop on the way at a good bookshop and spend £20 on her; he showed some reluctance but she reminded him that she would be shortly booking their Spanish holiday. And off she went to Court to deal with this errant husband.

CHAPTER 8

Late August

"Shura stretched out, admiring the young man who lay at her feet. The end to the week, escaping home and husband, flying free of roads, cars, any suspicion of pursuit, to the camp, their own camp, ..."

For goodness sake, Mary, she thought. What has happened to your writing? Where did all those intentions of being the latest Jane Austen go, the sharp wit set into incisive passages of domestic drama? All you seem to come out with is sex. Can't control it, can't restrain it; it bubbles through your veins and mind like hot pitch. Body and soul. Got to come out somehow. Frustrations, desires, Elizabeth, dominate your thoughts, actions ... Oh, to hell with it, leave me alone. She bent to the keyboard.

"... set deep in a small valley, the stream running through, wood for fuel. They had no need of food, had passed beyond that, except to bribe their young male slaves. They passed their days in peace, talking, exchanging experiences, playing music on their instruments, and using the men as slaves. The new ones, the women who were new to the camp, ah! They couldn't believe their luck; there had been complaints from the older members, the competition.

"The music was the drug, discovered by chance, like all great discoveries. An old man had come to their town, promising to teach rural instrument making. Men, dreaming of Stradivarius and French horns, had looked, scoffed and gone home. But some women had stayed, looked into his eyes and were drawn into a world beyond their own to a new freedom without restraints. They built their own instruments, simple, stringed or flute like, and all produced the sweet and subtle notes that seduced young men to forget their girlfriends, their duties and their homes, and to follow, as the Pied Piper of Hamlin was followed. They left the city at dusk behind the old man to leave their vehicles at some park, from where they flew to their valley. The young men were blinded, drugged and carried as cargo, slung below them. And when they arrived and settled, revived with music, they set to work."

Nice touch, the Pied Piper of Hamlyn. And women with women.

"There was no disharmony among the women;

after the greed of the newer arrivals, they were careful to limit the numbers and a pecking order was easily established, the older women having the first pick. Some were content to watch, play their tunes, stretch in accommodating nudity upon the soft grass while the sounds of satisfaction melded with the music into a symphony of completeness. They laughed and joked, compared each other's performance without rancour. One said that she had aged; they laughed in sympathy. The old man was among them, taking no partners, but talking, stroking, comforting, and playing. Indeed, he taught them new songs, new techniques upon their instruments that brought even higher skills from the young men."

Yeah, that's more like it. She didn't care, didn't care about the 'academic' writing, 'literary' and 'genre', or whatever it's called. Maybe there's a market for this kind of writing, she wondered. Lady's soft porn, as harmless as the Ann Summers shops on the high streets.

Mary stretched, smiled, and contemplated the next bit of writing; where could she go now? Must avoid too much repetition. It could wait; she needed company. That silly business with Elizabeth; Mari hadn't said anything when she came home. A little smug, some new books, a few clothes that Mary didn't recognise. There was no rush; she could still see Elizabeth for a time. Elizabeth had always seemed keen enough; Mary didn't think that she had disappointed her. And she had learnt so much. Felt as though she had been opened up with a can-opener, all the raw real her exposed and nourished. Wouldn't it be great to go away together? A weekend in an Italian city, lying in bed all hours, warmed by the sun, a stroll along the piazza, a glass of chilled prosecco, a light supper in the open, before returning to the bed, fall asleep exhausted much later, no snoring Daniel, and start all over again the next day. Wow. Why not? She felt that she must see her.

Nothing had been arranged, nothing said since their conversation that night a couple of weeks before. She hoped that enough time had passed, that Elizabeth had forgotten the pointless conversation and was feeling the same needs, the same desire to meet again, and again … She wouldn't want to give it up, not yet. It had only been a few months, nothing.

She picked up the 'phone; rang her home number – no answer. Elizabeth would be at work. Bugger. Not surprising really, these working 'professional' women. Elizabeth had said to never ring Chambers, unless there was an emergency. An emergency that must involve Edward and Daniel; or life and death. Mary thought about her excitement, dying in an empty house on a warm day; what a waste. An emergency. She dialled the Chambers number.

A quick reply, official, Queen's English with a hint of Cockney, male. Would it be possible to speak with Elizabeth? A still pause. Who is calling? A friend, Mary. A further pause. I'll see if she is in Chambers; she is very busy, she might be in Court. Please hold. The line went dead, cut off. No sound of typewriters, secretaries drinking coffee, chatting. Isn't that what went on in offices? There was a click.

'Mary?'

'Elizabeth. How are you?'

'Very busy. What can I do for you?'

'Oh Elizabeth, don't be cold. Do you have any free time today? I'd love to meet. I could be there in an hour or so.'

There was a pause; Mary tried to imagine what Elizabeth was doing, thinking.

'You know, Mary, we weren't going to meet anymore. You have too many problems, Daniel, Mari, family … it doesn't work.'

'But it can. There's no change, it's just us. Let's meet.' Mary feared that she sounded a little desperate and willed herself to be confident, a confident woman with an interesting life, travelling and talking of interesting things, attractive and … she looked around the hall. And shut her eyes, shut out the images of a busy family life, the boring reminders of washing and shopping and cleaning and mending. She didn't have to be that woman, the housewife.

'Let me buy lunch for a change, Elizabeth. Today? Or tomorrow?'

Now shut up, Mary, she said to herself, don't push too hard. It never works, sounds desperate, sounds sad. There was long pause; she couldn't imagine what Elizabeth was thinking.

'OK Mary, look, I have to go. Tomorrow, same place? 12.30pm. It's no good, you know. See you.' And she was gone. Mary hugged herself; it will be fine, she sung to herself, just fine. You wait and see, Elizabeth.

Mary watched the time passing, waiting. A whole day to be borne, a day to be wished past. Children, supper, Daniel; she did nothing that she did not have to, nothing to improve the home, cleaning, washing, shopping. She read, wrote and sat, gazing into the future, willing it to come to her. She knew what she would do when the time came, when the children were gone. She listened to her breathing, her heart; both raced. She felt contained, a wound-up spring in a still house. All was frozen; even the dust hung still in the hall, defying any logic of gravity. Still.

Flying out of the home, over rooftops, away still further, fields, mountains, thin air, flipping through space and time, any recognisable state of what was right and what was wrong was no longer supportable. Beliefs were balanced against weight of prime needs, and lost. Habit and chaos. A tilt to one side, the slightest gesture to upset, and overcome the years with a jump. She laughed.

'What is it, Mum?' Josh was in the hall.

'Are you ready to go? Where's your brother?'

'Yes, no, he's coming.'

The air settled as her youngest disappeared upstairs. She was looking out of the window; a bird settled on a bush, a hawk dived, took it, was gone; she saw nothing. A squall of rain rattled on the glass; her absorption in matters to come did not waver. A cockerel crowed, wolves flowed around the house, bison roamed and wild tribes fell upon her; she laughed, again. Sitting on the University Tower, dancing on the bones of tradition, a pole dance on the flagpole, spiralling float to the ground, young men in her path, high heels piercing the rolled lawns of esteem, clucking, sighing ...

At last, the boys were ready, ready to be dumped upon some poor housewife to play with their friends. That was good, to play with friends. Far better than staying at home with Mum or being taken somewhere boring, somewhere educational. They would be happy, fulfilled, fed, cosseted. It was enough; no, more than enough. Better than she could do for them today.

And no need to worry about Mari; away on some Cornish beach. There had been no card, no phone call. No problem. She wondered idly whether Mari had enough clothes, the right sort of clothes for a teenage holiday on the beach. Enough protection from sun and inquisitive eyes. She remembered her own youth, a few days at the seaside, Southend probably, a group of girls together, a mutual deterrence to the male scavengers who were scared off by taunts and blatant ridicule. Scared off so that there was never any risk; how innocent it all seemed now, changed for ever by the 60s, that came too late for her.

She hadn't talked to Mari about her London trip. She had welcomed her home as though Mari had been shopping. Mari had been cool, occasionally gazing at her with a wondering look. But Mary did not wish to open up a can of worms, to drag her affair into the open, expose it like a piece of road-kill. She wanted to hold it in her, a precious jewel to be preserved and cosseted. What right had her daughter to wrest her single precious thing away from her? A gulf grew between them and Mary looked forward to Mari's Cornish trip with a friend's family. She made no comment on the small bag that Mari had slung on her shoulder and bid her farewell with an effusive gushing of maternal love, hugging, hoping that she would have a wonderful time, not to bother to think of them. Mari gave her a strange look, wondering and worried but couldn't wait to get out of the door and into the car waiting at the kerb.

She was with Rachel; a solid family base, boring father, small brother, caring mother who was a good friend. But not the sort of friend with whom to discuss marital infidelity. At least, she didn't think so.

And Daniel? While he was being stupid, blind and selfish, he could manage his own life, provide for himself. She would be back later, she supposed. Sometime. Daniel could assume the family mantle, pick up boys, cook food and keep them company. Put off his other obligations.

She left the boys, not getting out of the car.

Watched them to the friend's door, a wave and was gone. To leave the car at home and take a bus into town.

The station; she knew it well now. It represented a translation to freedom; she wondered whether the Victorians who had built so many grand station entrances saw it in the same way. Gateways to another kind of life, to travel that exceeded expectations and took the passengers far beyond a day's travel that they would have been used to by horse, cart or carriage. The train took them to another place in a different time zone.

She knew it well – the ticket machine that didn't jam, the right platform, the coffee stall, a rare croissant to still her stomach. It was warm but she didn't notice whether the sun was shining or bother to plan which side of the train she must sit on to avoid the glare. She was absorbed in dreams. She felt that she was becoming a character in her own novel, a free woman flying away to fulfil her needs, to set aside daily duties and have her own time. She would fulfil herself, her life would come alive with …

A voice spoke near her; she blinked, stared without recognition. Someone who knew her. A woman, a little younger, wearing a business suit, some sort of badge on the lapel. A briefcase. What was she saying?

'How's Daniel? I haven't seen you both for ages.'

What was her bloody name? Couldn't remember. But she was University, some department or other. Professor or Lecturer or something.

'Fine, fine,' said Mary. 'Must go … got to …' She turned, a slight wave and hurried down the platform. Look busy. Toilet? No time. More coffee? Bugger it, she didn't want anything, only the train and London. She hid behind a large man; he was reading a newspaper. He smelt of sweat and stale cigarette ash. He looked down at her, a casual glance and returned to his paper. Mary ignored him, gripped her hands. Waited.

The train was late; no reason given. It was full and hot. She perched by the door and thought. How was she going to persuade Elizabeth? Make her realise that things did not have to change. After all, Elizabeth still wanted what she had started, didn't she? It was she who had started it, wanted Mary. So if the problems were all around Mary, Elizabeth could rest easy. They were not big problems. Just marital problems like anyone might have. Affair or no. And it wasn't as if she was threatening Daniel with a man, a lover who might become possessive in a marrying sort of way. Far from it. If Daniel only realised it was a case of two women gaining some satisfaction in the face of two husbands who apparently had better things to do with their time and energy. You might say that the two men ought to know better; pay attention to their marriage vows. You might say that the two women ought to know better, stifle their frustrations at the altar of marriage.

But for goodness sake, what century was this? Were they chattels to be directed by their husbands as the men wished? Time had moved on. There was this Feminine Lib thing, wasn't there? Mary was not too sure what the Feminists were saying, what bearing it had on her situation but surely it was all the same thing, women being free to live their own lives. It wasn't as if she was deserting Daniel or the family. Far from it; she was looking after herself. She would be a better woman, mother and wife because of it. Elizabeth had better stop this nonsense about Mary's family and get on with it. Or rather, get down to it. Mary giggled, remembering.

The train dragged through the late summer countryside. The oaks were turning black, dark shapes against the bleached gold of the harvested fields. Occasional fields of sugar beet looked messy, leaves drooping. Narrow dry lanes wound around the fields, disappeared over near horizons to villages with Anglo-Saxon names. It was all idyllic, pastoral, peaceful. A baler worked close to the line, dropping large round bales like dinosaur pooh.

Mary saw all of this and forgot it instantly; she had never had much interest in the countryside. Countryside meant no people and muddy distances between the few rural residents who inhabited this green desert. She couldn't understand Matthew's love of the wind-blown freezing hills and isolation. She thought fondly of past days when school friends crowded into coffee bars, chatting, comparing notes on lessons, parents, boys. And after, perhaps a quick trip around the shops before home for tea and homework.

Later, a gang of nurses in pubs, a comfortable group. And shopping with friends, the bustle of going into town, staying there for hours, a nice meal and dawdling back later than expected. By parents, or Matron, or husband, or children.

The train was late; a lame excuse. The driver hadn't turned up? Please, what century was this? Couldn't someone else have just jumped up there, switched on, driven down the tracks to London, putting the brakes on when necessary? At least you didn't have to steer, like a bus. There had been a girl at school who believed that train drivers steered trains round the corners; she had had a terrible time backing out of that one.

She bolted for the Underground. A queue at the booking office. At the front, a man had asked a question; he wanted to know how many changes before he got to Clapham. At the counter, the ticket man was looking for a map, a pencil and a pad to write directions. From Paddington? Mary found herself calculating the man's journey, the changes, the amount of time. She could tell him in two minutes. What was she doing? The queue became restless as it grew. She fumed, looked at her watch. It was time; time to be sitting down to lunch. Would Elizabeth be late? She doubted it. What would she say? It was a bad start; she had intended to be cool, a professional managing sort of woman who was never late, would take no nonsense, put her affair back onto its tracks. She wondered whether to take a taxi. She had tried it before; it had been slower.

She had her ticket at last. Onto the platform and not too long to wait. But after the train, it was still at least half a mile to walk.

The café was in a quiet street in Mayfair, not far from Shepherd's Market. Elizabeth had introduced it to her and it had become 'their' place where they always met. The proprietor recognised them, made sure that they had quiet table near the back, were served discreetly and were not disturbed.

Mary walked up to the door; she felt uncomfortable, her back sweaty and hot, irritated with the slow journey, and uneasy, nervous. Where had her confidence gone? How nice it would be to go straight to the hotel, strip and shower in company. It wasn't how she had planned to arrive; where was the calm assurance, the sexy smile, the casual lift to her shoulders, a sway to her hips? She clamped a tight smile onto her face, walked inside.

Elizabeth was sitting at a different table, at the side. There was a bottle of mineral water on the table, no wine or food. Not even olives. She got up as Mary walked in.

'It's very late. I need to go, work.' Elizabeth swept her bag under her arm and faced Mary. No kiss or hug; her face was blank, no recognition of familiarity as though she was a business contact. Mary's heart sank; it was going to be hard work.

'Please, the train was very late. I hurried. Please,

stay a while.' Mary sat down under Elizabeth's glare and signalled for the waiter.

The waiter hovered. Elizabeth looked at him, at Mary, sat down with a little sigh, a frustrated moue. Mary looked at her; what could she do? She had to change the situation, take charge. Without conferring, Mary ordered food, enough for two, and a bottle of wine, their usual white. It was delivered with speed, the spent bottle of Evian removed with a flourish. Elizabeth sat in silence.

Mary looked at her. 'How are you? Really? I've missed you.' A smile, an attempt at warm familiarity. And her heart beat an uncomfortable rhythm; she wasn't there yet.

'I'm fine. Very busy. We are trying to get away soon to Spain, our usual holiday.'

'Lucky you, it sounds lovely. We might get away to the Lakes again.'

'It doesn't sound as if you want to go.'

Mary made a face. 'It's not my idea of a holiday. I'd rather go away with you, just you, somewhere warm.'

'But that's not going to happen, is it?'

'You know, we have something special; something that we can't just throw away.' Gently, thought Mary, gently does it.

'We had something special. But you know very well, Mary, you can't go on. Not with your family up in arms.'

'Up in arms? It's not like that. Daniel does not have

time for me, Mari has her own life, and the boys are just innocent young boys. It's just one of the marital glitches. I'm sure you have them too. It doesn't affect us.'

'Of course it affects us.'

'No, that's not fair.'

'Don't be naïve, Mary.'

'How can you?' Mary felt she tears coming to her eyes; she brushed them away angrily. Where had it all gone in a flash? Elizabeth was unreachable; there seemed no way to make her understand. Oh God, how horrible.

'Do I have to remind you that I've known Daniel a long time? I would hate to be the cause of hurting him.' Elizabeth looked cool and appraising as though 'hating' had nothing to do with it.

'It's a bit late for that; you were the one that started our affair; but you were right; it has been very good. You've always been right, you've been marvellous.'

'Time to bring it to an end, though, isn't it? Now, I really must –'

'No, Elizabeth. I deserve a bit more than that. Do you remember the first time? I was so naïve, then. But you took charge.'

'I know, but –'

'I had no idea, did I? You taught me so much, and I never realised how good it could be, to satisfy and be satisfied.'

For a while, they were quiet, eating and drinking.

Mary assumed that they were both lost in memories. She hoped that she was winning Elizabeth over, after all, she was still here, and felt a renewed energy and looked for a softening in her face. Why did it have to be Elizabeth who called the shots? It was her turn now, her turn to seduce her, to bring her to heel. If only she knew how. She was aware that she didn't have Elizabeth's power of persuasion, making people feel that they wanted what she wanted. Her mind wandered back to the last time in London when they had tried out a toy … it was all so good. Stupid to throw it all away. She dismissed her dreams, sat up and spoke firmly, laying out a strategy, a plan for the future, a way forward.

'You have done so much for me and now I want to return the favour. I want to give you pleasure –'

'You can't talk like that anymore, it's too late.'

'But I can. That's the place where you took me, and you can't leave me there. I'm trained now, able to satisfy and bring a new –'

'Then, find a new partner.'

What? The thought struck Mary like an arrow of ice; another partner? Impossible. 'But I can't leave you.'

'There must be somebody at Reading, perhaps in the University.'

'No, you don't understand. How can you –'

'Mary, it's time, we can't go on like this. I've told you. I shouldn't have come today; I thought we could have a civilized lunch, be friends and move on.'

'But there is no need. Don't you still want it?'

Elizabeth paused, looking at Mary. Mary knew that they were bound to be friends in the future; Elizabeth was Mari's godmother and went to University with Daniel, whose best friend was Edward, Elizabeth's husband. It was inevitable; there could be no permanent break. Why couldn't their affair go on? Why couldn't they appear to be meeting for art trips?

'Goodbye, Mary.' Elizabeth stood, brushed down the front of her skirt as though brushing off all unpleasantness, picked up her handbag and was gone with a wave to the proprietor. Mary staggered to her feet, her mouth open. She grabbed her bag, started to talk to the waiter who had appeared, thrust a £10 note at him, and ran for the door.

At first, she couldn't see Elizabeth. The pavement was full of late lunch office workers, wandering on and off the pavement, meeting and greeting, smoking, loitering. Mary pushed through them, causing the occasional comment, a whistle, a shout. She pushed on and saw Elizabeth walking at speed ahead of her, men parting before her, staring a little. No whistles, no cat-calls for Elizabeth.

Mary ran. 'Wait, don't leave me.'

Elizabeth looked back, shrugged her shoulders, and waited.

'What are you doing, Mary?' She sounded genuinely puzzled, as though an old friend had just made an improper suggestion.

'Where are you going? We hadn't finished lunch; or talking.'

'I have to go; I have a con this afternoon.'

'No, please, don't leave me now.'

'Goodbye Mary.'

'No, come back. What are you doing?'

'Stop shouting, Mary. What do you think people –'

'I don't care what people think. Bugger 'people'. It's you I care about.'

'Really?'

'Yes,' she said quietly. 'O course it's you, I love you –'

'No, Mary, not me, you don't love me. You have had a good time and it's time to move on. Now. '

'It can't be, I'm not ready, it's too soon. I want you –'

'No, Mary. Life is not like that. It's time to go. Goodbye, Mary. See you soon, maybe up at Keswick.'

'Oh, I hate the Lakes. I want you here …'

Elizabeth had turned, and walked away.

Mary felt hot, her hands gripping her bag. Words tumbled through her mind, words that she had meant to say and not been allowed to utter. Words that would have changed Elizabeth's mind, put matters back where they belonged. Why could she never say what she wanted to say? Or was it that her words lacked the power of persuasion? She looked at Elizabeth's back, so sure, so perfect. Why? What had happened, in the space of three weeks? She discounted Mari's London trip; an uncomfortable accident to be brushed aside.

Could it be that Elizabeth had another lover? That

Mary was being dispensed with, an old lover no longer of any use? Mary was stunned; she hadn't taken that into account at all. Elizabeth couldn't have found a new lover so soon, could she? But she ran over their conversation at the café; everything pointed to it. Yes, that was it, wasn't it? So convenient, the story about family difficulties. A perfect excuse to move on.

That was why it was so sudden, this casting-off. The bitch. The blood roared in her ears, lost in the roar of the traffic on Park Lane ahead. The bitch; she wouldn't get away with it. She would accuse her, reduce her, bring her crawling back. Now she would see who was in charge.

She ran after her, slipping between pedestrians, dodging cars. At that moment, Elizabeth paused on the kerb, looking for a gap in the traffic. Mary crashed into her back, raising her hands instinctively at the last moment. Elizabeth fell forwards into the road. Mary heard screaming, shouts, a siren.

She ran.

Any direction, cannoning off bodies, walls, running through streets and alleys. Any direction away from there, away from the horror behind her. It hadn't happened, had it? It was a nightmare; she would wake, soon. But she had done it, hadn't she? And it was an accident, but her hands were up. She had pushed. Not intentionally, but she had pushed. And now Elizabeth was dead. Dead. She was a murderer. It was too late to walk away, make friends at a later date, even though she pined for her lover. It was too late to say sorry or persuade her to come back. It was too late to rescue Mari's godmother, Daniels' old university friend. She was dead.

Hours later it seemed, she stopped running. Her feet were sore. She had no idea where her silk scarf had gone, the one that Elizabeth had given her at their second meeting. It was a surprise that her handbag was still there, clutched on one arm. She was weeping, her face hot, throat burning, lungs aching. She curled into a heap on the pavement and allowed time to pass. Her whole body ached and she longed to lie down and forget everything. Become a vacant vessel, washed up on some strand of eternal forgetfulness. Some hope.

A voice broke through her consciousness. She turned and saw a policewoman bending over her. She was young, cleanly uniformed, an official concern on her face. For the first time, she wondered what she looked like; not a vagrant, not badly dressed or impoverished. But middle class, fallen on bad times. She stood up, a helping hand under her elbow. Did she want an ambulance?

'No, no, I'm all right. I've just had some bad news, that's all. An old friend.'

The policewoman smiled, offered help again. Told her that she couldn't really leave her lying on the pavement, it wasn't right.

'I'm sorry,' said Mary. 'I'm going now. Thank you, you're very kind.'

She straightened her clothes, wiped her face, and watched the policewoman walk away, occasionally looking back over her shoulder. It never occurred to her that the police might be looking for her, or that she might give herself up for murder. She felt exhausted.

She looked round. It wasn't warm any more. A brisk breeze lifted the litter around her. Where was she? It didn't look familiar. Mary didn't know London well, except for the East End and Central London. She asked for the nearest Tube Station. It was close. Got to get back home. What else is there? Home seemed a very long way away, and in the past; it could never be the same as it had been that morning. She saw Daniel and the boys as though through a thick glass window; watched them having tea, laughing and joking, her own place empty. She was not needed, not a criminal in their comfortable home. But where else could she go?

And what would she say? Pretend that she had been to London without seeing Elizabeth? Daniel would know, know that she hadn't been able to give up her affair. Perhaps he would know that he hadn't helped her to give it up, by spending more time with her.

The news would arrive, possibly this evening. By telephone. She could imagine Daniel going into a deep depression; perhaps he would go to Islington, keep Edward company. The three university friends, old friends, close. She didn't belong, never had. Would they let Mari in Cornwall know? She couldn't imagine telling Daniel what had happened. She probably would, in time; she didn't see how she could not. What else was there to do? She didn't think of the boys; they were in a different life, cosseted and cared for. She never gave a thought to when they should be picked up. There was always Daniel. He loomed over her thoughts like a god, judgemental and frightening. There could be no return to peace with him; he would be hit by the loss of Elizabeth and his best friend's loss. And by his wife's treachery.

What would she actually tell him? That Elizabeth had deserted her and walked off? That it was an accident, but admit that she was a murderer? How could she ever live with it? It was too much. She couldn't take it all in. She came back to the fact, again and again – Elizabeth was dead. And she had murdered her.

She walked to the Underground Station slowly, bought a ticket, wandered down to the platform. It was crowded. She was pushed aside in the corridors by commuters rushing to get home. She bounced off shoulders, walls and escalators. She followed her feet dumbly, stopping to work out the directions as though they were in a different language. An obstruction, she was spun around by the crowds. Time had ceased to be relevant; she was following directions dumbly, as an animal, not questioning motive or outcome. There was nowhere else to go, nothing else to do. Except to go home. Some sort of basic instinct, a haven at times. But this evening? How could it remain a haven? Get home; what for?

She found herself on the platform. Assumed that it was the right direction. It was full; she eased her way to the front and gazed at the track. Black and filthy as usual, with gleaming rails running both directions. Which was the dangerous rail which you must not touch? She didn't know. A rat ran below the edge of the platform; she bent over to watch it. It looked up at her, brushing its whiskers, and trotted on, stopping at an empty crisp packet, moving onto an apple core. Was it depressed? It looked quite happy, a warm home and plenty of food. Did rats have worries?

A man took her arm, warning her from standing too close to the edge. Pointed out the yellow line, better to stand behind it. She shook him off, frowning, hearing nothing. Men; they were not the answer to her problems. They were the ones that caused problems; wars and famine and violence, and frustration.

She backed away from him, to the front of the platform again. There was a roaring in the tunnel, flickering lights. At that moment, there was a surge in the crowd behind her as a fresh flood of commuters rushed for the train. She fainted at the edge of the platform as the train came into the station.

CHAPTER 9

September

The journey was long. In First Class, she was able to get some work done on a brief that the dear Clerk had been able to release early, earlier than the twelve hours before a con that was more common. She was not sure why she was going back to Keswick; there would be difficulties and embarrassments. She felt she owed it to Edward and Daniel, to be there with them. To share in the difficulties. It was comfortable on the train and after a good meal, she fell into a doze.

Matthew picked her up at the station; he looked well in spite of everything. She wasn't sure whether he knew much about that awful accident. A dark cloud hung over them. It was easy to look back and point to the moment when one might have acted differently, changed the course of history. She had done it many times in the last few weeks. She was curious as to how Daniel was managing; Edward was a little sad for

Daniel, of course, but he hadn't really known Mary well and Elizabeth suspected that he had never had much time for her. He was more concerned for Daniel. She saw a new side to him, after all those years – the degree of love and care for a friend. It surprised her.

And Elizabeth? How had the accident affected her? She had been shocked. Mary had been a close friend, a sometime lover; the memory of her clung like a cloak, coloured her thoughts. In a funny sort of way, she remembered her more clearly than if she was coming with them, her habits, her body. It had been shocking, the timing of it, just as they were finishing their affair. Did she feel guilt? What for? She couldn't see how the accident had anything to do with their parting. These things happened everyday, accidents and partings. She had thought it strange, the Underground Station where it happened; what was she doing there?

Dear Matthew, the life up here suited him. She wondered how his social life was progressing and whether he had acquired a partner or even a close friend. He chatted away, mostly about walking and exhibitions that he had seen, at Kendal and further afield. He didn't mention Mary or his visit to the hospital. He told her that the summer season had passed. The crowds had departed, returned to their schools, offices, factories and homes, and Keswick had assumed a quieter mantle, had been returned to the local people, with pubs, clubs and societies for winter entertainment. As they drove down from Penrith, cloud settled on Blencathra and evoked the romantic thread of the Lakes that was now part of him.

They arrived and sat down. He poured tea and was distant, at first.

'Edward has e-mailed me to say that he will be joining us at suppertime; he has gone to look at a house; I sent him the details. I know that is not how you want to spend your spare time; up here.'

'Matthew, dear, please don't worry about me. You are a good friend to Edward; he needs friends like you.'

'But, what about you? What's happening in your life?' He paused. 'It's not my business but we did talk in April and I have been wondering whether there is any resolution to this problem.'

'I don't think that we will resolve it,' she said, looking directly at him. 'We have grown apart, and I don't think that we have anything in common anymore.'

The time for feeling angry and awkward had passed and she wasn't embarrassed talking about it. On the contrary, she felt new horizons and opportunities opening and couldn't wait to explore them.

He looked struck, sad. 'I feel as though I was just getting to know you.'

'Come to Paris; do,' she said. 'I shall have time to go there now and I want to show all my friends the Paris that I love. My Paris. You would love it. I'm going to get a little apartment, perhaps share it with someone, and I have friends who live there already. You know, it is so easy. Next summer, I'm going to take my goddaughter there. You know, Daniel's daughter, introduce her to Paris and give her a taste of adult life. I can do that; it will help Daniel. Mari is growing up so fast, she has a mind of her own, and she deserves it. It will be fun.'

She remembered how it was Mari who broke up her affair with Mary and thought that Mari might provide her with a little compensation and fun through introducing her to cosmopolitan life. Poor Daniel, he wouldn't know her but it would help him if she developed a little independence, grew up a bit.

'I thought work absorbed your whole life. When you came up in June, I hardly saw you; you came in with the night and left at dawn.'

'Yes, well ... But I haven't given you my news. I am a QC now.'

'What does that mean?'

'I earn a hell of a lot more and can afford to pick and choose. No more driving offences, thank God. Juniors can do those. I can focus on my marital work. Solicitors get to hear of my reputation and I'm more in demand.'

'Well done! Congratulations! Let's open some champagne tonight, celebrate.'

'I don't want to rub it in Edward's face.'

'Don't worry about Edward; I'll look after him.'

Yes, she could see Matthew looking after Edward. But what about Matthew? How was he bearing up? He had lost his wife only two or three years ago and now his daughter-in-law was lying in a London hospital with serious injuries. No, she hadn't visited; she thought it would excite Mary and would delay her recovery. Daniel had suggested that Mary's mind had wandered a bit, whatever he meant by that. And how was Daniel?

'You're not lonely yet, are you, Matthew? It wouldn't be fair. Not that life is fair, but you know what I mean.'

Matthew seemed careful with his reply; she wondered if she had gone too far.

'No, not lonely; far from it, actually. But still learning to live alone. There is a crowd of good people here, a lot of single women, not so many men of my age; or at least, I haven't got to know them yet. You know how it is with married men; sitting at home with their wives, television, or out at supper parties with other married couples.

'But I have spent quite a lot of time with Daniel. They are still all at sea, no home organisation, except for a girl who comes in to do some cooking and cleaning, a sort of housekeeper. He's not doing well.'

'What about the children?'

'Too early to say. Mari appears the worst; silent, depressed. She even broke down once and told me that it was her fault. For goodness sake, how could it be her fault? She doesn't like to visit her mother, as though she is the cause of her accident. I don't know when they are expecting to return Mary home.'

Elizabeth looked away; did Mari feel guilty? That was awful, suggested she should feel guilty as well.

Matthew stared out of the window, brooding.

'Anyway,' he said. 'They're all coming up here this weekend. Be gentle with them. Especially Daniel.'

She left him in the kitchen and went to unpack. She had to share a room with Edward but slid the beds apart. While she was upstairs, she heard him arrive, sounding young and full of joy.

Downstairs, he gave her a brief kiss and turned back to Matthew.

'It's a jewel; you were absolutely right, just the right size in a good location. And not too much work to do. What a dream.'

She asked him about his new discovery, and he talked away, telling her about it and describing the alterations he had in mind. He looked so young, almost vulnerable; excited and full of his adventure. He reminded her of Oxford days, how he used to come bounding up to her like a puppy, smelling of sweat and the river. She was happy for him; and happy to be moving on from him.

'Have you bought it?' she said.

'No, but I'm going to put in an offer tomorrow. It's been on the market for six months but things are a bit sluggish at present. It belonged to an elderly couple; the family want to get rid of it. The agents seem to think that I won't have any trouble getting hold of it and didn't think that my alterations would be refused.

It's lovely. Not as old as I expected, but beautiful rooms and great views. Edwardian, I think. A lot nicer than Victorian. Not too much land with it but I don't want too much to look after.'

She wished him well. She could see him leaving London and working with a practice not far away. It would help her; they would sell the London house, provide her with enough capital to buy a flat close to Chambers and Kings Cross, and a fantastic apartment in Paris. She hugged him; he looked surprised and laughed, his relaxed flow of gurgling joy that had attracted her to him so many years ago. How times had changed since those early Oxford days. But no regrets, no wanting to patch up their impossible differences.

Matthew poured wine. And they sat and dined in the sort of peace and contentment that she and Edward had not shared for a long time, talking of Oxford and their future apart.

Around nine, Daniel and the children arrived. They looked tired as they flowed into the house, dropping bags and walking boots. The boys were loud and restless, released from hours in the car. They were glad to be with Matthew again, asking for expeditions and outings. He took them into the kitchen and shortly afterwards, upstairs; the chattering died away.

Mari wandered in and stood staring around; she looked exhausted, her eyes glassy. She ignored Edward and looked at Elizabeth; for a moment, she looked as though she might speak. She turned to the stairs and slowly went up, bearing her bag and a weight of grief and unspoken words. They heard Matthew greet her on the landing. There was silence and Matthew came down after a while.

Daniel had dropped down in front of the fire, his coat still on. He had ignored Edward and Elizabeth. Matthew looked at Daniel.

'You must want something to eat.'

'No, nothing. Just a drink. Whisky?'

Edward had been silent, watching Daniel. He sat down next to him, close. Elizabeth decided to leave the two of them alone. The peace that had dominated supper had vanished. She went into the kitchen; Matthew was gazing into the distance, an ice tray dripping in his hands.

'I don't know what to do. Daniel ... no, not now. Goodnight, Elizabeth. Tomorrow ...'

She took the ice tray out of his hands and filled the bowl. Helped him finish the tray, carried it into the livingroom. And said goodnight to Edward and Daniel. She was asleep before Edward came up.

Nobody enjoys those difficult times when a parent is in hospital for a long time and it is difficult to communicate with the patient. Daniel had been shocked by the telephone call and departed for London after finding a very obliging friend to care for the children, feed them and see them off to school.

And at the hospital, Mary had been in a coma and he had sat there for hours, the doctors unable to give him any information until Mary surfaced and they could carry out investigations; eventually the nurses had gently pointed out that Mary would be unconscious for a long time, and he should go home. Didn't he have family to look after? The University had vanished from his thoughts but began to slowly reassert itself; there were telephone messages waiting for him at home. The good neighbour had told a caller that Mary had had an accident and the information had filtered through to his faculty. He found it difficult explaining the situation to his children. At first, the boys were tearful and didn't know how to deal with the information; when was Mummy coming home? How did she have an accident in an Underground Station? What was wrong with her? When could they see her? Mari would not talk to him at all; she vanished into her room and didn't reappear for meals. Daniel had no idea what to do; however, Rebecca's mother sent Rebecca over to talk to her. It seemed to improve things and after a day or so, Mari came to meals, silent and withdrawn.

Elizabeth woke early and sat up. Edward was asleep in the other bed, his back turned to her. She looked out of the window; heavy clouds chased up the valley towards the town, full of rain. She tried to sleep for a while but soon gave up and went downstairs.

Alone, she marvelled at Matthew's house. The

1930s style architecture seemed dynamic, fresh, space sweeping around the staircase and the fireplace towards the kitchen. She saw parallels with the hills, how the sky swept down the valleys, was forced over cols and stopped at the head of corries, dissipating over tarns and lakes. How unlike Matthew, she thought. But then, how well did she know him? Vague past memories of their house in Leeds summoned up an image of narrow Victorian architecture, small separate rooms, leaded windows, panelled study, heavy bath and basin in an old-fashioned bathroom. But here, all was openness and light. With few walls. The house was quiet, a faint smell of wood smoke and wine, cool.

She stepped into the courtyard; the paving was wet, earth colours glowing in spite of the dull light; the walls, brick and stone, encrusted with moss that flowed from the joints, were tumbled with plants. In raised beds, blanched rose petals curled to the earth. She shivered, looking up at the hills that stood over the town. And felt alone. Perhaps it had been a mistake, coming here. Perhaps there was nothing to be resolved, no help to be accepted. She should go, leave them all to come to terms with their tragedy.

Matthew appeared; he looked rested.

'It's a dull day, isn't it? What would you like to do?' He gazed down the valley, wrapped in his thoughts. Through the window, she saw Daniel; he was perched on a chair, his hands thrust into his pockets as usual, staring at her.

'Give him some space, eh? He'll be all right in a while.'

'Can I –'

'Better not. He just needs space.' Matthew went indoors, shut the door firmly behind him, and disappeared into the kitchen. Elizabeth stood in the yard, hugging herself. She was cold.

They gathered for breakfast. Edward sat by Daniel, chatting about nothing in particular; Daniel gave a few replies, eyes down. The boys sat around Matthew, asking what they were going to do; one pulled out a map, suggesting a hard route over rock and hill. Matthew looked, laughed, and suggested something easier. Mari came down last, looked at Elizabeth, ignored the spare place laid next to her and sat down at the far end, drawing up a stool. Elizabeth was isolated; nobody spoke to her or wanted anything of her.

After breakfast, she found herself alone with Daniel. She moved next to him; he gazed at the table.

'How are you, Daniel?' she said.

He looked at her, his face frozen. And said nothing.

'I'm sorry. I'm bitterly sorry. About Mary.'

'Don't!' he said, suddenly furious. 'I lost her to you. The family lost her, and then the accident … we never had a chance.'

'But it was over –'

'How could you? After all the years I've known you? Why, Elizabeth, why?'

Elizabeth thought about Mary's complaints about

Daniel, how he never gave her any time or attention, turned up late for meals, was always out of working in the evenings. She wondered briefly how much of it was true; had Mary been creating a fiction to suit her needs? It was quite possible. Or was it just an exaggeration? After all, Edward worked all hours too. She knew how it could be.

'I'm going, you know. I came up this weekend to say goodbye to you all. Edward and I are separating, and I thought that it would be good to be together once more –'

'Together? How can we be together, without …' He turned away.

'We've known each other for so long. Can't we just be together, say –'

'Was I such a bad friend to you?'

'It happened, you know … we both wanted it … I can't describe it …'

He gazed at her and she remembered how he had looked at Oxford, always the serious student, scruffy with a frown and a look that focussed miles away.

'Do you remember at Oxford when …' She stopped as Daniel got up and left the room. And sighed. Perhaps he would come round one day.

Matthew and the boys went for a walk, saying that they would be back in the afternoon; the boys looked impatient, keen to be away from the others, the constant reminder of their loss. They were booted, anoraked and carried rucksacks, proper walkers and proud of it. Edward sat down with her, showed her the details of the house that he wanted, and went off into town to make an offer. He took Daniel with him. He seemed happy with his change in life, looking forward to a new home in the Lakes. She could imagine him finding a wife, perhaps a divorcee with children. She thought he might be a rather good father, missing out the awful baby stage. She wondered whether it would be a happy marriage. She sat alone, thinking about getting back to Penrith Station. Feeling that she might as well be enjoying herself in London.

Mari came downstairs; Elizabeth had assumed that she had gone into town with the others. She sat down opposite Elizabeth, her hands gripping the edge of the table. She looked drawn, but was becoming more attractive than ever. Her wild hair had been cut and she was dressed in a beautiful white shirt with jeans.

'You're angry with me,' said Elizabeth.

Mari was silent.

'You knew about our affair, didn't you?'

Mari started to cry.

'I'm so sorry about her accident. The affair; it had ended, you know. Because of you and Daniel, and the –'

'Did you do it?'

'What?' Elizabeth was confused.

'Push her. Were you there?'

'No, I was in Chambers. We met for lunch, just lunch, as friends, and –'

'So she did meet you.'

'Yes.'

'And then?'

'We parted. I had a con and she walked off. I don't know where.'

'How was she? Had you had an argument? What happened?'

'No, nothing like that. I thought she was going home; I have no idea how she ended up at that Underground Station. Unless she had gone to see someone, a friend or something.'

'I thought, perhaps –' Mari scraped at her face with a tissue.

'No, she was good friend.'

A pause.

'Daddy is in a frightful state.'

'Yes.'

'I don't know what to do. I wish ... I wish I could make things different for him, you know, ...'

'You can't, can you? But you can help him.'

'How? What can I do? I feel awful, I think I'm responsible somehow, I caused it –' Her fists were gripped, tears dropping on the table.

'Stop, Mari.'

'I –'

'Stop that, now.'

'But –'

'I know, it's awful.'

'I miss her, terribly. And I wish I had been nicer, or better, or –'

'No, Mari, you were fine; you are fine. You are a special person and I know that Mary was very proud of you. She spoke often of you.'

Mari broke into loud crying, folding up on her chair. Elizabeth went over to her, knelt on the floor, stroked her hair. After a while, the crying stopped. Mari jumped up and went into the kitchen. There was a loud sniffing, the sound of the kettle boiling, and she came back with two mugs of coffee. They sat in silence, and the sun shone, birds sang, and time passed.

Mari looked up. 'It's not very easy at home. The girl is a frightful cook and has no idea. She's only a student. All heavy greasy food. Daniel is getting fat, when he remembers to eat. The boys never have clean clothes, and –'

'Can I help? Let's do something about it, shall we? You and me?'

Mari stared. 'How? Can we?'

'If you'll let me. If Daniel will let me.'

'I don't know; he has forbidden the mention of your name in our house. I'll talk to him. What could we do?'

'There are agencies, and things like that. For cleaning and cooking and so on. And we could go shopping, together if you want.'

Mari stared. Elizabeth could see her thinking, whether she wanted Elizabeth in her life, how she would handle her father. What her choices were, how to make life better for the family. And she wondered how much time it would take, and whether Daniel would accept it. He might want to cut the connection between godmother and goddaughter. That would be a pity.

Elizabeth smiled and looked at her. She would have to handle Daniel with kid gloves. She would take Mari in hand, help her to manage her home and get into university. And she would take her to Paris. She owed it to Mary.

They went into town, looked at shops, bought a few clothes for Mari, lunched in a teashop and arrived home shortly after the boys and Matthew.

And Elizabeth told Matthew that she thought it best if she left them, and she was going to ask Edward for a lift to Penrith Station. Matthew looked at her, at Mari and the boys, and told her that he wanted her to stay, at least until the next day.

That evening, Edward was in high spirits, unable to hide his excitement. His offer had been accepted. He had no fears of finding work, converting to a rural existence, perhaps a small firm, a big change from his London life. Even Daniel seemed infected by it, smiled occasionally, and stayed close to him as though warmed by Edward's happiness. He appeared happy to dispense with his children; his father had taken the boys in hand, and Mari had attached herself to Elizabeth. She saw him eyeing up his daughter with a wondering gaze.

The boys ignored her. She didn't mind; they had never related to her and followed their grandfather, occasionally spending a little time with their father.

Supper was an early meal. As usual, Matthew insisted on cooking; he enrolled his two young assistants and could be heard teaching them how to cook. Occasionally, there were shouts, as one boy or another criticised his brother and tried to take over; a quiet murmur from Matthew brought quiet. Daniel drank heavily; Edward watched with a look of concern. At table, Elizabeth sat at one end with Edward on one side and Mari on the other. Mari hardly spoke to her when others were present, beyond polite enquiries about holidays, and passing the pepper; she distanced herself from her brothers. At home, did she attempt to take their mother's place? It would be a struggle. When the boys asked for wine, Matthew looked at Daniel, who shrugged his shoulders; they received a small glass each, competing with each other and knocking it back as though it was Coca-Cola.

After supper, Mari helped Elizabeth clear the table and Matthew asked them all to come outside to his studio. They stood in silence in the courtyard around the studio doorway, the boys restless, inquisitive. It was cool, quiet. There was no traffic noise and the skies were clear, early stars appearing on the horizon. Elizabeth shivered. Matthew opened the double doors, dragged an easel forward to the doorway, and pulled a sheet off the canvas.

It was a large painting, by Elizabeth's standards; an unframed canvas about three feet square. A landscape with a broad view, it looked towards a range of mountains, possibly Blencathra and Skiddaw. A slope in the foreground fell away to a lake on the right, with a path rising towards the foreground, on which there were four walkers. At first, Elizabeth thought she was just looking at a Lakeland view; she wondered why Matthew looked so hesitant. A minute passed; silence. With a shift of perception, she realised that the four figures were the four of them, Daniel and Mary, Edward and Elizabeth, and that Matthew was showing them his private view of his friends and family.

It was clear that Matthew knew much of what had happened. Elizabeth looked more closely. Daniel, in sharp dark colours, was shown striding forward, his hair flowing in the wind; Mary, a little rounded in warm browns, was on his left, a little behind as though struggling to keep up, but within grasp. And on Mary's left, close, was Elizabeth, sharply delineated, bright walking anorak singing against the sombre background colours. Edward was apart, the other side of Daniel but further ahead, walking as he always did, setting the pace. As Elizabeth saw it: Daniel and Mary, with herself placed ambiguously close to Mary, and Edward far from her striding his own path.

There was silence; Elizabeth was amazed; she had no idea that Matthew was so skilled. She wanted to ask him how he had become such a good painter. And when he had accumulated so much information, the faces, the attitudes.

There was a choking noise. Daniel turned, his face twisted, mouthing words, tearful, and shooed his boys away. Matthew looked distressed, followed him with his eyes.

'I wanted to show you all.' His voice was hesitant, long pauses. 'It's my record ... of the four of you ... my record of the four of you walking together.' He stood still, staring at the ground. Slowly he began to pull the sheet over the canvas. Edward stopped him. Elizabeth looked at Mari.

She was staring at the painting, her mouth slightly open, eyes full of tears. She moved close to the painting, taking in the details as though to absorb them into her skin, to bring the image to life. Matthew watched her; his face was open, alarmed as though she might strike him. She turned to him and stretching out her arms, took him into a hug, breaking out in tears. Elizabeth touched Edward and they withdrew, back to the house. There was no sign of Daniel or the boys.

'I wish I could tell him,' Edward said. 'It's really very good. A wonderful painting, you can see what's going on, and it's very good of the mountains. That's Blencathra, isn't it? I like the figures; he seems to have got us pretty well.'

Elizabeth was not sure whether Edward had taken much notice of the figures, whether he saw the particular grouping that Matthew had painted.

'I wonder if he would sell it to me,' he said. 'It would look good over my new mantelpiece.'

'I should think that Matthew will want to keep it. He said, it's his record.'

And she turned away from Edward, who was staring out of the window at the picture that Mari and Matthew were covering.

On Sunday morning, Elizabeth tried to leave again but Matthew would not have it.

'The early trains are rubbish and I think that Mari needs you. Daniel ... well, Daniel is not himself, just now. And there's the boys ...' He turned away, preparing breakfast. His two helpers were with him. Daniel and Edward appeared later.

After breakfast, he suggested a short walk. They squeezed into Edward's car and travelled the few miles up to the little car park on the hill to walk up Coledale. The wind was slight but cold, from the northeast.

Matthew was walking with Daniel, talking at length as though to persuade him of something. They ignored everybody. Edward had gone ahead, as usual; the boys tried to keep up with him, occasionally breaking into run. Eventually, he relented and they walked on either side of him, chatting away without listening to him. Mari and Elizabeth followed behind. They talked. Mari was reading newspapers now and had the confidence to express her own opinions and tastes. She challenged Elizabeth, about her life style and her work. And asked her if she did any charity work, or had been to any Third World country.

When they had walked for an hour or so, Matthew stopped and they stood together looking forward to the mine at the head of the valley. The boys wanted to go on but it was cold and the mine was still a mile ahead. They turned and started to walk back. Mari attached herself to Matthew; the boys sought out Edward, taking the lead again. Elizabeth found herself beside Daniel, who was looking calmer, a distant look in his face. He looked away from her, across the valley to Outerside.

'I've always loved this valley,' he said. 'No roads, no houses, and then ahead the mine on the col. It would be nice to go up to Grasmoor one day, bit of a climb, but you'd have the views over to Buttermere and Crummock. I know, not much of a walker but I think the boys would like it. Have to make an effort for them.'

Elizabeth thought he sounded like his father; it was a surprise to hear him so calm, almost distant.

'I have to –' she said.

'Don't, I don't want to hear it.'

'Daniel, I don't want to leave things like this; we have known each other a long time. Mary is my friend too; I miss her. Can I help you …'

She faded into silence as he stared at her. She wondered if he was all there.

'I could do things for you, home, shopping, that sort of thing –'

'Leave us alone, Elizabeth. You have done enough damage for the time being. Give us a break.'

Elizabeth remembered the blow in her back as she waited at the kerb on Park Lane. She knew who had pushed her. But it wasn't important, just a petty angry gesture. She had fallen forward, a big step into the road, the nearest car swerving, braking as the man next to her pulled her back. Funny that siren, just then, like a clarion call. She sighed.

'Goodbye, Daniel. I hope everything goes well and you have Mary back soon. I'm leaving today.'

And she walked on alone, leaving him behind. Perhaps Mari would get through to him. No point in pushing a boulder up a hill, to watch it roll down on her.

When they returned to the house, the others sat round the fire, coats on, looking like a group of crows hunched together. Nobody looked round. Elizabeth was excluded. She went looking for Matthew and found him in the kitchen.

'Before I leave, could I see the painting again? It was amazing. I had no idea that you were such a good painter; Daniel has never mentioned it and I can't imagine when you have had the time.'

'Oh, I've always painted. You know, Sunday afternoons. Always been keen on landscape painting. And we had a great City Art Gallery at Leeds. I trained myself, I suppose. Had more time for it since moving here, when I'm not out. Walking.'

'The hills, your inspiration. It must be wonderful, the connection between the two. Have you sold any paintings?'

'No … no, I'm not good enough for that. They're all in the studio. Get them out sometimes, remind myself of places, you know.'

'Could you show me?'

'Hang on a minute. Boys …' He called to the boys, asking them to get lunch ready, and turned to go outside. They ran into the kitchen, barging each other at the doorway. There was an explosion of shouting, a crash. Matthew sighed, passed the studio key to Elizabeth.

'I'll join you in a minute. Stick to the new painting, could you? Gently when you take the sheet off.' And he turned into the kitchen to engage with the boys and restore peace.

Elizabeth slipped outside. She felt excited to be allowed to see the painting alone without distraction. In the studio, the easel stood at the centre, draped liked a memorial. She lifted the sheet clear of the oil paint gently, allowing it to fall to the floor behind. The light was not good. She searched, found light switches, and turning, felt a glow of colour hit her as if the canvas was on fire. She smiled, enjoying the raw feeling.

She stood back to take in the whole picture.

Her breathing stopped.

A gush of pain hit her as though she had been punched in the stomach, squeezing tears into her eyes.

Near the centre of the canvas was hole, about nine by six inches. The centre stretcher bar appeared behind the gap, straight and alien. The edges of the hole were ragged, as though a small sharp blade had been used in a hurry. Through the hole was the darkness at the back of the studio. Missing from the picture were the two figures, Mary and her. On the trolley next to the easel was a mass of paint tubes, bottles of medium, pots of brushes, rags, trial pads, pallets. And a Stanley knife with canvas threads caught against the handle. She gasped, pulling air back into her lungs. And stood, staring.

She didn't know how long she stood there. She ran through all the motives that might have existed in the house for destroying the painting, every individual, and could not conceive of any suspect. She noted the evidence, the raw cuts and the Stanley knife. The door had been locked, no sign of forced entry; not an outsider. Therefore no police and no fingerprinting, not here. A crime scene that could not be investigated; judgement would be left to suspicion and bias. Like earlier centuries.

She even wondered whether Matthew had destroyed his own painting, after Daniel's grief and anger. She considered opportunity, the only persons who had had the time, unobserved, to take the key from the kitchen and slip outside. And realised that it was her; she had had the best opportunity, early in the morning. Always the first up, and she knew where the key was hung. But she had not done this terrible thing. Had Daniel been so distraught?

The door opened behind her and Matthew came in.

'Ah, at last ...'

She looked at him, her throat dry, unable to say anything. Like her, he froze, staring at the hole.

Interval, an empty hole in time. A bird called, a car passed on the road.

He gulped.

'Why? Oh, ... why?'

'It's terrible,' she said. 'Who would have wanted to?'

He was silent.

'Could it have been somebody from outside? A burglar?'

He was silent.

'Surely, it wasn't –'

'Why?' he said. 'Why, Elizabeth? I don't understand.'

She was silent. Thinking.

'Why?' He looked puzzled.

'Perhaps,' she said, 'it was Daniel? After last night?'

He looked at her, eyes disbelieving.

'Well,' she said. 'He was very distressed by it. I don't know –'

'How could you? Why, Elizabeth?'

She stared at him.

'Why, Elizabeth? And how could you blame Daniel, my son. After all...?'

'Why would I –'

'I don't understand you. What possible motive could you have for ... for ... doing this?'

'No, Matthew, I haven't ... couldn't –'

'Tell me. Please.'

'But, it wasn't me –'

'I need to understand. Why did you do it? Some hidden envy, spite, possessiveness? What?'

She was silent. Dumb. He turned to the trolley, picked up the Stanley knife, looked at it, held it out to her, accusing, wordless.

'Yes, I saw it,' she said. 'And –'

'And you used it. But why?' He was becoming unbalanced, a tide of grief and control that he had been exercising for the last weeks overflowing. He waved the knife at her, as though he might slit her open to find the truth.

'Please, Matthew, I didn't do it.'

'And who would have done it? Who? And I gave you the key, I trusted you, the studio has been locked since yesterday evening, I assumed –'

'It wasn't me. Please, put the knife down.'

'First Mary, then Edward, then Daniel, now me. Whose life do you want to tear to pieces next? Mari?'

'What? Tear lives to ...' Tears were coming to her eyes. She felt a great sadness, and anger. It wasn't right, that was not how it had been. How could she ...

Matthew was suddenly calm, as a river freezes over.

'Get out of here. Leave now. I don't care how. Leave

us alone. I thought you were my friend, our friend. I don't…'

He stopped, turned his back on her. And started to rip the canvas, showering pieces onto the floor, a harvest of bright unreal leaves.

'Go now, please.'

She went back to the house, collected her bag. Nobody spoke to her. Edward said that he would take her to Penrith; didn't seem surprised by her sudden departure. She looked at the others gathered round the fire; Daniel didn't meet her eyes, gazing away. The boys stared. And Mari gave her a little hug, without a word, and turned away.

At Penrith, Edward gave her a polite kiss, cheek to cheek. He would be back in London, but giving in his notice. Making preparations to leave, putting the house on the market. He asked if she had everything, smiled, left to drive back to Keswick.

She had to wait for two hours for a train. In the waiting-room, she opened her case, looking for a file to read. Work was a constant, always settled her; she was able to remain remote to the feelings of her clients, to be their counsel, do the job, move on. An intellectual challenge, the Courts her playground.

She frowned; everything had been disturbed, turned over. Her shirts were crumpled, skirts askew. Somebody had been going through her things; had they hated her that much? And when had this been done? She started automatically to straighten things, the case laid open beside her. A pile of clothes built on the bench, as she refolded, to pack properly from the bottom up. Nothing appeared to be missing; she couldn't understand the random intrusion.

At the bottom of the case was a polythene bag, flat. Not hers; it looked as if it came from a Keswick supermarket. She laid it on her lap and slipped her hand inside. And slid out a section of canvas, the canvas with the two figures.

Why, she wondered. Who. The figures looked up at her. They looked as positive and vibrant as they had last night, and memories came back of that walk. The walk above Derwentwater, a bright Spring day when the world was young and fresh, grass recovering from the snow on the hills, the air sharp and invigorating. Conversations, a happy time of togetherness, Matthew often in front, his camera in use as usual, looking around, forward, back, the skies and the lake. Were they accusing her, haunting her now? Was this some bizarre revenge by Daniel, or ... who else?

A piece of paper drifted to the floor. A shopping list. Potatoes, butter, eggs, sugar, oats, aspirin, veg ... she turned it over.

"Elizabeth, I don't have much time. Please could you keep this for me. Daddy was very upset by it. See you soon. Love, M."

Ah, Mari. Her Mari. She saw a split in the family, Mari turning to her, Daniel and Mary and the boys apart, a future that would need navigating with care. And Mary; what would she feel?

She replaced the canvas and the note, put them in the bottom of her case, repacked her clothes, and chose a file. For a while, she gazed out of the window, looking through present time to the future, through recent problems to a clear time. Then she opened her file.